AMBER ARGYLE

DAUGHTER OF WINTER

FAIRY QUEENS 6

First Edition: April 2016
Library of Congress Cataloging-in-Publication Data
LCCN: 2016905925

Argyle, Amber
Daughter of Winter (Fairy Queens Series) – 1st ed
ISBN-13: 978-0-9857394-8-5

TO RECEIVE AMBER ARGYLE'S STARTER LIBRARY FOR FREE, SIMPLY TELL HER WHERE TO SEND IT:
http://eepurl.com/l8fl1

Outshine the darkness.

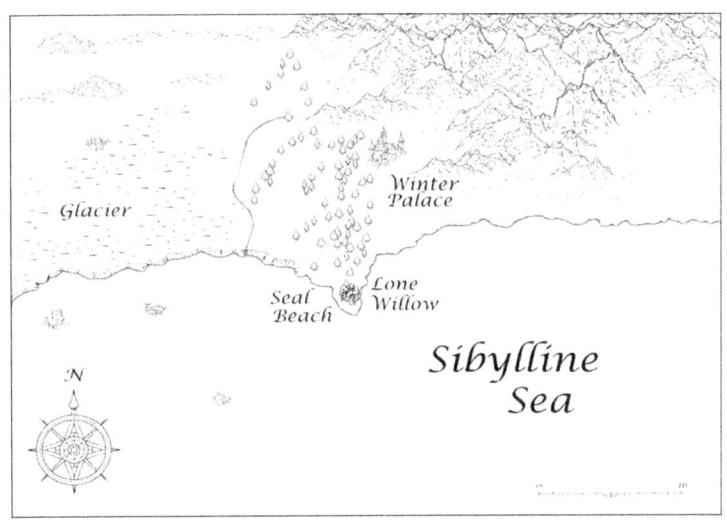

Glacier

Winter
Palace

Seal
Beach

Lone
Willow

Sibylline
Sea

N

1

The horizon was a brilliant orange when Elice slipped out of her cave wearing only a white linen underdress. The crystallized snow felt rough under her bare feet as she ran through her forest of ice sculptures. Before her was an ice tree that, when the wind was just right, became a wind organ. There were animals, too, all with prismatic features. An owl was startled to flight from its high perch by two reindeer, antlers locked and mouths open.

Breathless and hungry as she always was after the darkness, Elice left the forest behind and paused where ice met black ocean. The light grew brighter until she had to squint. But she didn't look away, not until a ball of gold peeked over the horizon. She grinned and stretched her bare arms toward the pale sky, letting her skin soak in the sun she hadn't seen in six months. It caressed her as she breathed it in, tasting sunshine that spread through her body and chased away the shadows that plagued her.

The wind picked up, tugging playfully against her hair, thick and so dark it was almost black. She could have stayed that way forever, but there wasn't much time left to find food for Picca, her injured seal. From inside one of her trees, Elice retrieved the belt she'd weighted with stones. She secured it around her waist and then opened herself up to winter—like pulling open a window to a storm of ice and snow. She tugged on a trickle of that power.

Shaping the ice as it flowed from her hands, she quickly encased her head in a clear bubble, which she sealed against the skin of her shoulders. She formed flippers on her hands and feet, picked a spot between the circular ice floes that littered the water, and jumped into the ocean. The weight of the belt pulled her down to where sea plants shifted with the current. Inside her bubble of air, Elice took in the shafts of light piercing the water's rippled surface and then refracting below. It was like being inside a giant, one-dimensional prism. Before her, the ice floes of the Winter Queendom stretched on in an almost minty green. Behind her was the small peninsula she shared with her family, the ice palace built beyond the shore and tucked into the steep mountains.

Unlike the unending silence of the queendom, the ocean was alive with sound—the chucks, whistles, chirps, and booms of seals and whales. Here, life flourished in a way it never would above. Careful to make sure her ice bubble didn't separate from the skin of her shoulders and allow the air to escape, Elice swam up to a small octopus, killed it with a shock of cold, and stuffed it into a large leather bag trailing from her belt.

After tying off the string, she looked up and came face to face with an enormous walrus, its tusks the size of a two-handed sword. Elice tensed and opened the window to winter a little wider, forming an ice spear in one hand. But the walrus simply twitched its whiskers and swam curiously around her. Then, as if it had lost interest, the creature moved away, its tusks ripping at the mollusks embedded on the rocky sea floor.

Elice exhaled in relief. Swimming away from the walrus, she searched for more prey. In the distance, she could make out a silverfish wriggling in the space where an ice spear stabbed down from a floe into the ocean. The fish's mouth busily worked free whatever food it had found. Spear still in hand, Elice moved smoothly toward the fish. But she hesitated before swimming over a boulder covered in sharp-edged mollusks and a hundred different water plants.

On the other side, the sea bed dropped off sharply, leading to open water. In the distance, the water was red with krill. A dozen too-thin leopard seals hunted the swarm. Though Elice had the magic of winter at her fingertips, she wouldn't dare come near a group of seals that were twice her size. Besides, hunger had made the seals even more aggressive than usual. There were other dangers too—the orca that hunted the seals and ruled the open waters.

Still, she didn't have much time, and the silverfish was the only other prey she'd seen. Steeling herself, Elice left the shelter of the shallow water and pushed toward the silverfish—a somewhat misleading name, as it was actually a salmon pink. The creature only turned silver after it died.

Elice had just gathered some of her power when something exploded above her. A dozen large-eyed seal pups plunged into the water, tails frantically pumping. Elice didn't wait to see what had panicked them; waiting could mean death in the queendom. She swam hard for the shore. In her peripheral vision, she saw a polar bear diving into the water after one of the pups. It opened its huge mouth full of sharp teeth and snagged the baby seal. Blood curled through the water, and Elice pivoted and kicked out. Even she dared not face a hungry polar bear.

In her panic, she had separated the ice bubble from her clavicle, and now water filled the bubble to her chin. Her head felt light and floaty—she'd taken too many breaths. She glanced around to ensure that nothing else was after her before she kicked for a distant ice floe. Just as she surfaced, she drew the ice back into winter. Taking hold of the raised, icy edge, she gasped in a breath of crisp air. She heard the seal pup squealing in pain as the bear dragged it back onto the ice. Elice's first instinct was to try to save the pup, but it was already too late. Besides, the bear had to eat, just like she did.

Trying to block out the sound, Elice let the spear and shield dissolve from her hands. She looked back at the faraway shore. The winter palace and her forest appeared no bigger than she was. She glanced into the watery sky to check the time and was surprised to see smoke rising in the distance. She stared. Here, she was the only one who lit fires.

Curious, she pulled herself out of the water and onto the higher vantage point of the ice floe, doing her best to ignore the sound of the bear ripping and tearing at the seal carcass. The scene was distant enough now that Elice could cover it with her outstretched hand.

Floes from the spring melt stretched into the distance. Dominating the horizon was a chunk like a floating mountain broken off a glacier. The smoke was coming from behind the iceberg. *Smoke means people,* Elice thought. She'd never known other people. Never met anyone outside her immediate family.

Hope and longing tore at her. But with that hope came fear, for after six months away, the Winter Queen was returning today. And she would never allow a ship to survive this close to the queendom.

Knowing running would be faster than swimming, Elice dissolved her flippers and opened wide the channel to winter, letting water freeze beneath her feet as she ran across the ocean, ice spreading just ahead of each of her steps.

Her heart pounded in her ears when she finally reached the iceberg, her underdress and hair hanging stiff and heavy from her body. She withdrew the cold, and they were wet and dripping again. She climbed the steep ascent and peered over the rise.

Elice gasped in disbelief at what she saw—a ship, close enough that she could make out dark-skinned men running about in panic, shouting to each other. Elice gaped at them. She'd only seen three people in her entire life, and here was a whole group of them!

She squinted and read the name etched in the side of the ship—*Drauga*. She'd never laid eyes on a ship in real life, but from her books and her grandfather's stories, she knew what it was. This one was obviously damaged, for it leaned sharply to one side, a trickle of smoke coming from somewhere below decks.

Movement in the sky drew Elice's gaze. A flock of ice fairies shifted in the air currents like a school of fish, their clear-as-glass wings catching the sunlight in a thousand sparks. They hovered between Elice and the ship. Dread seeped into the place where hope had been. She was too late. Too late to meet the ship. Too late to warn its occupants.

Tinted green by the water, a spear of ice shot out, stabbing into the underbelly of the ship. The ship's scream sounded remarkably close to the cry of the dying seal pup just a few minutes before. The men released a small boat, but the moment it hit the water, it was crushed between two ice floes.

Having completed their dark task, the fairies fluttered away, leaving the craft in her death throes as they headed toward Elice. She knew their destination was the Winter Palace, and she was directly in their path. She ducked down, pressed herself flat, and tried to keep her breathing shallow. The fairies passed over her, their wings making a sound like a hundred scissors opening and closing at once.

Elice wanted to stay put until the fairies were long gone, but there wasn't time. Whatever they'd done to that ship had doomed it—otherwise they wouldn't have left it. She eased around the other side of the rise, putting the iceberg between herself and the fairies and hoping her movements hadn't caught their attention.

A horrible screeching of wood made her whip around. The ship canted to one side before plunging into open water again. It was listing badly and sitting heavy. Water gushed out some sort of pump, but the craft was sinking fast now, water closing around the sailors. They began to scream.

Still at the pinnacle of the iceberg, Elice sent out a ribbon of slick ice. She sat on it and slid. Her wet hair whipped behind her, freezing in crazy tangles. She wasn't fast enough. Helpless, she watched as the ship slid beneath the surface, dragging the men down with it. Some of them splashed around in the water, but with their heavy fur clothing and their weapons, they sank faster than the ship, which was already fading like a ghost.

When Elice reached the edge of the iceberg and launched to her feet, all that was left behind was a bit of flotsam—shards of wood and barrels ripped loose from their moorings. There was no trace of the sailors. Hands crossed and pressed hard over her mouth, Elice silently waited for one of the men to resurface. For someone to have survived. She couldn't explain the tears that pricked her eyes. All her life, she'd been taught that humans were insignificant, their deaths no more important than the seal she'd seen killed earlier.

But Elice dove in anyway, forming flippers even as she kicked and stroked to where the ship had been. She dove down, pushing away debris and hunting for any signs of life. She hadn't taken the time to form an air bubble, so she soon surfaced, panting. Then a man burst up on the other side of the debris. He gasped for breath, his hands tangled in rope wrapped around a barrel. Their gazes locked, and the shock of looking into a stranger's eyes rendered Elice temporarily immobile.

He was shivering violently, staring at her with despair. He made a shuddering sound again, as if trying to call for help, and she remembered that while the water was pleasant for her, it would be freezing to him.

"Swim for the iceberg," she cried even as she swam toward him.

He gave another great shudder, his lips moving as if he uttered a prayer, and kicked out. Whether he was trying to reach the iceberg or her, Elice wasn't sure. But then he slipped under the waves and disappeared. She dove below the surface and swam hard for him. His eyes were closed, and strands of his tied-back hair wavered in the water like sea plants as he sank gently into the water's dark embrace.

She grabbed under his arms and hauled him upward. They broke the surface, and she struggled to keep his head above water. She managed to drag him to the sloping edge of the iceberg, but with his multiple layers of dense wool clothing, she could not drag him out of the water.

Opening herself back up to winter, Elice let in a trickle of ice, which she formed into a razor-sharp point on the tip of her finger. She cut through the soggy outer layers of wool, pushed them off the man's arms and legs, and let the clothing float away. He was left with only a thin piece of cloth around his loins. She hauled his limp body onto the ice, noting how cold his skin was. She drew the cold away, back to winter. His color improved quickly, from ash to deep brown, and he moaned.

Elice's mother had been a healer before she became the Winter Queen, so Elice knew a lot about healing. She inspected the man, awkwardly running her hands over his bare skin. His arm was twisted at a bad angle. No wonder he hadn't been able to hold on to the barrel. He also had a hard lump on the back of his head.

He opened his eyes and looked at her again. His eyes were so warm, like cinnamon flecked with black. Through bloodless lips he mumbled something Elice couldn't understand. She drew the cold into herself again, knowing she must get him out of the weather—to her cave where she could hide him. She had no doubt that her mother, the Winter Queen, had sent her ice fairies to sink that ship. If she found this man alive, she would kill him.

2

As the man mumbled incoherently, Elice opened her connection to winter and let ice flood through her. Using her hands and her thoughts, she shaped a small boat. Then she made herself a ramp, took hold of the man under his arms, and heaved. But though he was wiry, he still far outweighed her. She couldn't get him over the gunwales. Drawing in the cold that invaded his wet body, she clasped his face. "Can you hear me?"

When he did not respond, she slapped him hard. He blinked at her, but his eyes didn't seem to be focusing. "Find her," he said in strangely accented Clannish, gripping Elice's arm so tightly she nearly cried out.

Whoever he was looking for, she was gone now, lying at the bottom of the ocean. Elice pushed away her pity and ordered, "Stand up."

The man tried to bat her away. "Must find her!"

Elice growled in frustration. "I'm taking you to her. You just have to get in the boat."

He looked at the boat, then back at her, his behavior reminding her of when she found her grandfather so deep in his cups he could barely stand. Pure determination steeled the sail-

or's features, and he strained to rise. Elice helped balance him when he got to his feet.

"Climb in," she managed, breathing heavily. He tried to lift his leg over the gunwale and promptly tumbled into the boat. He didn't let go of Elice, who fell on top of him. Through her thin and sopping-wet underdress, she could feel every ridge and plane of his body. She immediately scrambled off. He groaned in pain, his hand going to his head as he curled into a shivering ball.

At the back of the boat, Elice leaned over the side and stretched out her hands. Snow stormed from her palms, building up under the boat and launching it into the frigid water. She shaped an oar and rowed them toward the Winter Palace, using ice to clear away the floes and pulling the cold from the man whenever his muttering started to fade.

When they reached the shore, Elice formed more ice beneath the boat, leveraging them up and out of the water. Then she pulled the ice back into herself. She tried to get the man to stand again, but his legs trembled and buckled. He collapsed on all fours and mumbled, "I have to find her." His lips were a dark gray, his skin damp and cold. Elice could draw out the chill, but she could not produce heat—his own body had to do that. The fact that it wasn't meant his systems were shutting down.

She took hold of him under his hairy, damp underarms and tried to pull him up. "Come on. You have to walk. I'll help you." He strained, but his good arm wobbled and he collapsed. "The girl. She's this way. I'll take you to her," Elice pled, the lie tripping off her tongue. Thankfully, the man seemed too disoriented to notice.

After some struggle he got one foot under him, but it refused to bear him up. He collapsed again, and this time he didn't rise. Elice pressed shaking fingers to his throat. His pulse was weak and sluggish, and he wasn't even shivering anymore. She glanced at the sky and noted the horizontal movement of the sun as it inched along the skyline. It wouldn't be long before her mother arrived. Elice couldn't drag the man all the way to her cave. He was too big.

She had been in this place before. If she had been stronger, it wouldn't have happened. And now it was happening again. She fought the panic bursting inside her. She gripped the man's shoulders and glared at him. "You are not going to die."

He didn't respond. Her mind spun, trying to come up a solution, some way to save him. With a pang, she remembered her father taking her sledding as a child, the runners gliding effortlessly across the snow. Concentrating her thoughts on the sled her father had made for her, Elice formed a replica of it directly beneath the man. She didn't have a way to pull it—ice was too brittle to function as a rope. So she tore off the hem of her underdress, wrapped it around the sled's handle, and started pulling, her feet digging into the snow until she was running.

The forest of ice blurred as she ran through it, dodging a razor-sharp porcupine, ducking beneath a shining spider web, and destroying a dandelion gone to seed. She kept glancing at the palace, waiting for the bells to announce the arrival of the queen and her court.

Elice was gasping breath into her burning lungs when she finally reached the entrance to her cave and plunged into the snow-lined tunnel. A couple dozen running steps and she was inside the cavern with its rough walls, bare rock, and sealskin-lined floor. It was by no means warm inside the cavern, but it rarely froze.

She settled the man next to the cold fire. Her only other patient, a fluffy seal pup, chirped hungrily at her. Ignoring Picca's cries, Elice drew the cold from the man again before rooting around for her flint and striker. Once she finally found them, she set about building up a fire, her haste making her movements clumsy.

When a few eager flames finally licked up the tinder, she added a few sticks of her precious firewood, brought all the way from the Summer Realm, and turned back to the man. She tucked a sealskin rug over him, wishing she had something cleaner. She didn't have much need for blankets.

Her underdress and hair had frozen again, so she melted them with a thought, then tugged the damp waves behind her ears. From one shelf she snatched balm, from another a brown tincture. She eased the man's head onto her lap and poured the tincture into his mouth. He choked and then swallowed reflexively. After settling his head down again, Elice smeared a generous amount of balm onto the lump and bandaged his head with a snow-packed water skin. He moaned and mumbled as she worked, which she took as a good sign.

She added more wood to the growing fire and was relieved when the heat pressed against her right side. The man tossed a little, but settled when she took her hand away. His coloring was better, his skin flushed from the heat of the fire. She turned her attention to his twisted arm. Upon closer inspection, she realized his arm was fine but his shoulder was dislocated and swollen. Elice had dealt mostly with animals, but she could guess what the joint looked like. She braced both her feet on the side of his chest, then gripped his hand and pulled.

There was a satisfying pop and the man reared up, screaming and clutching his shoulder. Elice scrambled back and smacked her head on the table behind her. Hand over the smarting spot, she watched him warily, her fingers itching to form a dagger. She'd been so frantic to save him, she hadn't even considered that he might be dangerous.

Holding his arm to his side, he fixed his eyes on her, then said something in a language she couldn't understand. The language was somehow familiar, but his words were too sloppy for her to place it.

He was shivering violently again—a good sign. Then it hit her with a sudden force: *he is going to live.* She had saved him, but she didn't know anything about him. Was he a good man like her father and grandfather, or a bad man like the ones her mother was always warning her about? And perhaps most important of all—what was she going to do with him?

Keeping her movements even, as she would with any injured animal, Elice reached up to the table behind her and took hold of one of her tinctures. She held it out to the man and said, "Drink this. It will help with the swelling." Hopefully the vodka and poppy would knock him out. *That will give me time to decide what to do.*

He accepted the bottle, sniffed its contents, and took a small taste before throwing back the whole thing, his throat working as he swallowed. Then he wiped his mouth with his good hand and looked around her cave, at the shelves filled with bottles and baskets. At the table made of whale bone lashed together with rawhide and littered with dry herbs. And then he focused on the sealskin rug that had settled on his lap.

"Well, it's not every day a man wakes up nearly naked in a beautiful woman's . . . lovely home," he said slowly in Clannish. Elice gaped at him as he gingerly settled down again and pulled the rug over him. "My ship?" he said, teeth chattering. She shook her head. His eyes squeezed shut. "And those on board?"

She stood up and put the table between them, then came closer to Picca, setting off the seal's chirping again. "You were the only one I found," she told the man.

He let out a sharp breath.

If he finds out who I really am, he will hate me for what my mother did to his ship and those onboard, to the girl he obviously lost. Best to keep my mother's powers secret for now. "Who are you?" Elice asked softly.

"Adar. I'm the navigator. I don't . . . what happened?" He looked her up and down. "What's your name?"

"Elly." She wasn't sure why she gave him the nickname her grandfather had chosen for her.

"My shoulder?" Adar said.

Elice undid the weighted belt around her waist, then removed the octopus and fed it to Picca. As the seal ate, Elice stroked her soft fur. "Dislocated. I popped it back in."

Adar ran his hands over the bandages on his head before checking the cord that tied back his shoulder-length hair. "Where are my clothes?"

"At the bottom of the ocean." Elice stepped carefully around him, put more wood on the fire, and took out a basketful of skeins of ripped cloth. "Your shoulder will feel better if we wrap it."

He gave a tight nod and sat up. "Do it." She took a skein in one hand, but hesitated as she stared at his bare chest, at the corded muscles and curling hair. There were scars everywhere, silver against the dark of his skin. One scar was as large as her palm on his right side. How had he survived that wound?

"Are all men as big and hairy as you?" Elice asked.

Adar turned laughing eyes to her. "No. Some are smaller. And hairier."

She swallowed. "Just so you know, I can kill you as easily as heal you."

He cocked a lone eyebrow, and she forced herself to rest a hand on his opposite shoulder. His skin was soft, but the muscle beneath was as hard as stone. Biting her bottom lip, she angled the strips of cloth down under his elbow and brought them back up. "Who . . . who is the girl you were looking for?"

Adar's brow furrowed. "What?"

"You said you had to find a girl. What happened to her? Was she on the ship?" This was none of Elice's business. Why had she opened her mouth?

His jaw tightened. "I haven't found her yet."

Elice wasn't sure what that meant, and she daren't ask more questions. She tied off the strips and took out another. "Lift your good arm." He obeyed, and she pinned his injured arm to his ribs, her fingers skimming his ribcage and causing him to shiver.

She tied off the last of the strips and gently pushed him down on the rug. "How's your head?"

"I've had worse," he said lightly. "Listen, Elly, I need to get out of here." She opened her mouth to tell him that was impossible—he was still shivering violently and hurt—when the palace bells pealed. "What's that?" he asked in alarm.

She glanced toward the tunnel. Her mother and her court had been spotted. It was a day Elice had both longed for and dreaded since Ilyenna had left six months ago, but now . . . Elice passed a hand over her mouth, studying Adar. If her mother found him, he'd be dead and Elice would wish she was. *Why did his ship have to come today of all days? Why couldn't he have shown up a week ago?*

She could turn him over to her mother. Elice would be punished, but it would be bearable. Yet at the thought of the life draining from this man's—Adar's—eyes, she shuddered. "You have to stay here, and you have to stay quiet." She pushed to her feet, hurried past him, and put more wood for the fire within his reach.

She snatched an armful of sealskins from the floor and piled them on top of him, wondering if it would be enough to protect him from the cold. She wasn't sure, but it was the best she could do. "The Winter Queen is coming. She will kill you if she finds you here. And she may kill me if she finds out I helped you."

He took a sharp breath. "Then this is the Winter Palace?"

"How could you not know?" Surely mortals knew never to trespass this deep into her mother's queendom.

"It's known that the palace is somewhere in Svassheim. But not even the Svass know where."

Elice knew of the Svass people, of course. Though she had never seen them, her mother insisted she speak the language of the neighboring highmen, who resided firmly inside the elastic border of the Winter Queendom.

Adar started to sit up again. "I have to go. There's another ship out there. I have to warn them."

Elice held him down. It was surprisingly easy, considering his size. "You go out there now and you're dead. You're safest here. They don't come into this cave—the fairies hate being trapped underground almost as much as they hate smoke." Her mother included. "I'll be back as soon as I can. Try to rest."

She started to stand, but Adar grabbed her arm. "Are you their servant?"

Elice hesitated. "I am the queen's ward," she lied. "I'll be back as soon as I can."

After donning a crumpled overdress from a corner of the floor, she buckled her clan belt around her waist, grabbed one of her old capes, and swung it around her shoulders. All her finery had been left in her rooms in the palace, and there was no time to retrieve them now.

She hurried, running so no one would get annoyed enough to come looking for her and discover her new patient. She cleared the mouth of the cave and skidded to a stop. Her mother and grandfather stood at the edge of the ice forest a couple dozen steps away, her mother's arms crossed impatiently. Hundreds of thousands of fairies fluttered at her back.

Trying to compose herself, Elice continued at a statelier pace. At first glance, mother and daughter looked very similar—both had black hair and fair skin. But where Ilyenna's eyes were a deep brown, Elice's were hazel. She had her father's fuller bottom lip and more rounded nose, too.

"See, Ilyenna," her grandfather said. "I told you she'd be along." His hooded eyes twinkled as he leaned on his cane, his white beard trailing nearly to his waist. His bald scalp shone in the sun. He wore clansmen clothing—a belted overshirt and undershirt, simple trousers, and boots.

Elice stopped just before her mother and bowed. Ilyenna reached out to draw in the cold from her daughter's frozen hair.

It flopped against her back, and her underdress was damp and sagging again. "Why are you not properly dressed? Where is your headdress?" Before Elice could answer, her mother sniffed. "You reek of smoke."

Elice's shoulders sagged. "I was trying to dry my hair."

"You can turn the water to snow and shake it out easily enough," her mother said, then did just that.

Feeling the sting from her mother's fingernails, Elice dropped her gaze to her bare feet. "I like the warmth. And snow never works as well as the fire."

Her mother pressed her full lips into a thin line. "Did you forget that today was the beginning of Winter's End?"

On the first day of Winter's End, they exchanged gifts and shared a special breakfast together before the formal ceremony with the fairies. Then followed two weeks of gifts—often simple things like stories and homemade presents given sometime throughout the day. On the third day, Elice's mother always provided them a feast with the fruits of summer.

And before it had even started, Elice had shown up in her swimming underdress and thrown the entire routine behind schedule. "No, Mother," she said finally.

Ilyenna took a deep breath and held it, as if calling upon her patience. "Don't let it happen again." She motioned to one of the fairies. "On this, the first day of Winter's End, I gift my father a book of Luathan history. And you, my daughter" —the fairies came forward, carrying a single bunch of frozen flowers between them— "I bring you lilac flowers."

Elice took the bouquet. They were clusters of star-shaped flowers in a cone form. It was hard to tell with the dusting of frost, but she thought they might be a pale purple. She felt herself softening a fraction. "Thank you, Mother."

Otec gave his daughter a carving of a frog with beady eyes. Then he said, "Elice, I'll need your to help to fetch your gift from my rooms."

She forced a smile. "My gift for both of you is on the other side of the ice forest." Without another word, her mother pivoted on her heel and passed under the icy branches.

"Has the war gone that badly?" Elice softly asked her grandfather.

Otec's gaze flicked to the fairies with their cold, unfeeling eyes. "We'll discuss it later."

"We're behind schedule as is," her mother's disembodied voice called back to them.

Elice took a deep breath, opening her connection to winter, though not to use it. She just wanted the comfort her magic gave her. She slipped her arm through her grandfather's to help him keep his balance and stepped into her ice forest. This section of the forest held new trees and creations she'd made since her mother left for the battle front. Ilyenna barely glanced at them as she walked purposefully through the forest.

Elice touched each one as they passed—a curling tree with clear-as-glass branches that cradled perfectly formed, opaque air bubbles instead of leaves. An enormous tree with glass drops dripping from its boughs instead of leaves.

"This one is rather . . . unusual," her mother said dryly. "Have you not studied the books I bring for you? The leaves are not in the shapes of raindrops."

Elice's shoulders tightened. "Grandfather told me a story of sitting under a tree long after the rain had stopped, yet the drops continued to plop on his head." It was one of the stories that filled her during the vast dark of midwinter, when the sun and its light would completely disappear for nearly six months, leaving them in perpetual night. "Besides, this one isn't your gift."

Her mother made a noncommittal sound in her throat. She paused before the likeness of a deer. It was all angles, from the sweeping antlers to the pointed nose and feet. "I'm certain I gave you a book about deer, too."

17

Elice stared at the creation that had taken her days to get right. She remembered the way she'd felt as she'd formed it—like she was all sharp angles. "Grandfather told me that animals adapt to their environment. I thought, what if a deer could actually survive here? What would it look like?"

Her grandfather reached out with a liver-spotted hand to touch one of the razor-sharp antlers. "I think it would look exactly like this." He hadn't seen this one before—hadn't seen most of what Elice had made over the long winter. It was a long walk from the palace, and he had come out less and less over the last year.

"I shall have more books brought in for you instead of flowers," Elice's mother said. "That way, perhaps, you will understand the subject better." She snapped her fingers, and one of her fairies flew off toward the palace to do her queen's bidding.

Elice balled her hands into fists. "My gift is this way," she said to her grandfather, ignoring her mother altogether. She strode through the forest, then climbed the steep glacier at the tip of the peninsula and winding up to where the pinnacle jutted out over the sea. There, standing alone was a solitary tree, this too was all sharp angles. She'd tinted the trunk black. The twigs hung like long streamers with crystal-clear prisms instead of leaves tinkling in the wind. A weeping willow. She'd liked the name. Though it wept, its leaves trailing like frozen tears down its branches, it was beautiful.

Her mother only sighed at the gift.

"My queen," said an ice fairy with clear-as-glass wings. "Lowl wishes to meet with you before her address. She said it is of vital importance." Lowl was her mother's general. Elice hated her.

Her mother arched her back. Purple and green wings, the color and shape of an aurora, burst from her shoulders and stretched to fill the horizon. "Come, Father, we're already behind schedule." She pumped her wings and shot into the sky, the fairies trailing after her.

Elice watched her go. She was glad of it. Glad to be alone with her grandfather. Guilt immediately followed. But anger shoved that guilt aside.

Her grandfather rested a hand on her shoulder. "She's your mother and she loves you. She just doesn't see the world the same way." Elice folded her arms over her chest and looked out across the sea without actually seeing anything. Her grandfather sighed and pulled her around to face him. "Where Ilyenna sees facts, you see possibilities. Someday she will understand that your way of seeing the world is a gift and not a burden."

The bells at the palace pealed again. The Winter's End ceremony would begin shortly. Elice gritted her teeth as she watched her mother disappear into the open-air throne room without a backward glance, the details of her lost to the distance. "Lowl gives that speech every year. And it's always the same. Every year, we get closer to winning. But we never really do. I hate it."

"Elice," her grandfather softly reprimanded. She dropped her head. He brushed the crook of his gnarled finger down her cheek and then stepped into the net her mother had left behind— only one net, not two. It took a few thousand fairies to carry her grandfather, and they were all waiting, their movements erratic with their impatience. "You best hurry. The ceremony starts soon and your mother hates it when you're late."

Elice debated telling him that her gift wasn't finished yet. When the light hit the tree . . . but she turned away instead. "You go. I'll be along later." He hesitated, and she knew he was deliberating whether or not to push the issue. But then he nodded to the fairies, who lifted him up and toward the palace.

Elice simply waited. She'd started this project the year before, marking exactly where the light crossed the pinnacle of the glacier and hit the spot where she stood. Alone, she watched the tree as the sun crept into view, bathing the tree with a rosy light. One by one, each of the thousands of prisms inside the tree lit up in smoky sparks, shooting fractured light all across the newly fallen frost, which she'd laid down last night. It glittered like the dusting of a thousand diamonds.

3

Elice slipped into her cave and found Adar asleep under a pile of sealskins next to the fire, snoring loudly. The tincture—laced with a bit of opium—had worked. She tossed a few more logs on the fire and checked on Picca, running her hand down the back of her head as the pup arched into the touch. The octopus wouldn't be enough; Elice would soon have to find more food for the seal. At least she was finally starting to fill out. The seals in the wild seemed to get thinner every year.

With a sigh, Elice crossed to the opposite side of the cave to stand before an ice relief that looked like a great tree with snowflake-shaped leaves. She took hold of one of the boughs and pulled. The hidden door swung inward, revealing a narrow staircase she'd created herself from densely packed snow. She slipped through the door and shut it soundlessly behind her. Already behind schedule, she rushed up the stairs. At the top, she paused to glance out the glass peephole before opening a door exactly like the one at the bottom of the stairs. It swung open soundlessly, and she entered her room on the third floor of the palace.

Her feet shushed softly across the clear ice floor, dusted with just enough snow to give traction. Frozen beneath the perfectly clear ice were layers of an elaborate snow fractal that gave the room a feeling of depth and delicate texture. The walls were made of opaque ice in grand arches with lacy pinnacles. Between these arches were more high reliefs, some more primitive than others, but Elice's grandfather had made her promise to leave a few of her more childish efforts. She yearned to fill them with the colors that hollowed her with longing, but all the skill in the world couldn't make her materials into something they were not.

She had made and remade the walls over the years, trying to match the picture in her head. High mountains capped by glaciers and rimmed by a thick texture of conifers took up three walls. The reliefs opposite Elice's bed showed steep hills full of wavering grass. If you looked closely, you could see a man swinging a sickle in one. In another was a flock of sheep, the animals herded by a young man—she'd added that more because of her grandfather's stories than to try to match the picture in her head.

And there, in the center relief, was a distant village, the walls made of round river stones, the roofs of split shingles. It was the village her grandfather and mother had grown up in— Shyleholm. Her grandfather had described it in perfect detail so many times that Elice swore she could taste the fresh-cut hay, could feel the sunshine, heavy and golden and filled to the brim with laughter. In her imagination she was always running toward something. But she never reached it.

She shook herself. Now was not the time for silly fantasies. She shut the door behind her and strode to a long table filled with vases of flowers. Elice quickly formed another vase and settled the frozen flowers inside. She hurried to her trunk and pulled out her nicest underdress and her overdress trimmed in white fur and embroidered with silver thread. She pulled on the underdress and then the overdress, which was shaped like a long thin blanket with a hole for her head. She secured it with the clan belt her mother had made for her years before, stitching the story that was Elice's life in the knots of the belt and adding a hidden leather pocket for her clan knife.

Elice felt the sensation of someone watching her. A few moments later, a tiny knock sounded at the door. She started guiltily, remembering the man in her cave, and the rules she was breaking by helping him. "Come in."

Set inside the door, a small fairy door opened. Chriel flew into the room. "Oh, I'm glad it's you," Elice said in relief. Chriel was a rabbit fairy, her furry wings pure white. She had bulbous pink eyes and a round face. Though all fairies were immortal, Chriel had an unusual aura of age and wisdom.

She smiled—a completely foreign expression for fairies, but Chriel had long ago figured out that it put humans at ease. The fairy landed on Elice's shoulder and settled down, her soft wings brushing Elice's cheek. "The books your mother brought are stacked in the library."

Chriel was the keeper of the histories. She'd insisted that Elice have books—that she learn to read and write and speak many of the languages of the world. Chriel had taught her everything herself. Such interest in a human, and a child at that, was unheard of among the fairies. Elice didn't dare bring attention to the oddity by questioning it. Chriel was, after all, the closest thing she had to a friend.

The fairy left her perch on silent wings. Elice bent down to slip on her soft leather boots, then stood over a short table topped with a silver bowl. With one touch, she melted the water. Then she glanced at her reflection—her wavy hair was a mess of salty tangles. She doggedly attacked it with her gold comb but gave up halfway through and wove it into a messy braid, which she tied off with a lime-green ribbon Chriel handed her.

"Anything special this year?" Elice asked, holding her breath.

Chriel hovered in front of her. "The usual. Books on plants and animals. Another on the Balance." She grinned a little, revealing pointed rodent teeth. "And an atlas."

Elice nearly went cross-eyed trying to focus on the too-close fairy. "Really? Oh, Chriel, you did it! You convinced her!" Elice would finally, finally know what the world looked like.

Chriel landed on Elice's head. "Actually *you* did it, by offering to make a dimensional replica of the world in the floor of the throne room."

Elice wanted to run straight to the library and memorize the atlas, lose herself in the world she would never see. "Maybe they won't notice if I don't come to the Winter's End ceremony this year."

Chriel didn't answer, and Elice glanced into her reflection. The fairy stared out the window, her wings stiff, her expression almost . . . sad? Fairies were never sad. Angry, gleeful, cruel, but never sad. "Chriel? What's wrong?"

"Can you feel it?" the fairy whispered, meeting Elice's gaze in the water's reflection. "The magic teeters on the precipice of change."

Frowning, Elice opened herself to winter, as she had done a thousand times before. The power was there, raging as always. But it did seem a little off, like too-thin ice beneath her feet. She cocked her head to the side questioningly.

Chriel's wings quivered. "The ice is already melting, breaking up. It shouldn't do that for another month, at least. The snow isn't as deep. The bears, the seals, the birds—they suffer for it."

Elice had been treating sick animals all her life. It was impossible to miss that there were fewer of them. More died every year; Picca was proof of that. "Mother says it's because of the Summer Queen's attacks."

"She would," the rabbit fairy said.

"What is it, Chriel?"

Chriel turned to her, her eyes brighter than normal. "Do you remember what I told you? What you have learned?"

"Which part?" Elice quirked a smile, trying to ease Chriel's gloom. When the fairy didn't answer, Elice sighed and then recited, "'Everyone has light and dark inside herself. Outshine the darkness.'"

"Promise you'll be at the ceremony?" Chriel said. "I'll be the one telling the history, and you need to hear it."

Elice perked up. Chriel usually had one of her under-fairies tell the story, even though she was the best storyteller. Something about being too busy for ceremonies. "All right. I promise. But are you sure you're all right?"

Chriel lighted from the chair and headed toward the door. "I will be. Soon. The Balance always has a way of righting itself."

"Chriel!" Elice called after her. "That wasn't much of an answer." But the fairy just disappeared through her little door without bothering to shut it behind her. Elice started after her but then realized she'd forgotten something. She hurried to the bust and donned the headdress made with seamless links of silver with opals hanging below her ears and the back of her head. Another opal draped her brow.

She dashed out the door, leaving her elaborate room and entering the bland whites and grays of the Winter Palace. She rushed through the grand corridors, down the wide, curving stairs at the rear of the palace, and thundered into the kitchen, where she promptly skidded to a halt. There sat her grandfather, Otec. Steam rose from a carved wooden mug in front of him. In the kitchen, only the walls and floor were ice. Everything else had been carved by her grandfather's rough hands—hands that had once been strong and deft, but now seemed too big for his shrunken frame.

"Grandfather, we don't have time for breakfast. The ceremony has already started."

"I can't stand Lowl's warmongering any more than your father could. And you're already late. We should have something to show for your mother's ire."

Elice edged toward the door. "I promised Chriel I wouldn't miss her history."

Her grandfather looked over the rim of the ice glasses she'd made him. "Then you best eat fast."

Letting out a sigh of consternation mixed with relief, she plopped down on a chair with carved leaves and branches painted in bright colors.

"Chriel won't start without you," her grandfather said.

"It's not Chriel I'm worried about," Elice mumbled as she studied the bowl of porridge flavored with bacon grease—a treat her mother had brought them for the start of Winter's End. It had congealed into a greasy, lumpy mess. Elice lifted the bowl to her mouth. The first swallow stuck in her throat, nearly making her gag. Suddenly she realized she now had another mouth to feed. After the ceremony, she'd have to sneak some food from the kitchens for Adar.

"It would have been hot if you hadn't been late," her grandfather said. He turned the page in the book he was reading. "What took you so long?"

"I had to get dressed." Elice glanced at the title and reached for the book. "Is that one of the new ones Mother brought?"

He pulled it away from her grasping fingers. "Yes. And you can have a turn with it when I'm done."

Elice had read her entire collection of books over the winter and was craving something new—specifically, the atlas in the library—but it would have to wait. "What's it about?"

Her grandfather eyed her. "I thought you were in a hurry."

Biting back a groan of frustration, Elice swallowed a couple more mouthfuls of porridge, quickly so as not to taste it. Her grandfather went back to his book. "Why were you so late to meet your mother and me this morning, anyway?"

"It wasn't my fault this time." She'd had to save a drowning man.

Her grandfather's eyes lit up in amusement. "You always say that."

"But it really wasn't. There was a hurt animal." Adar was, technically, an animal.

Her grandfather sighed. "You can't save every injured creature you come across."

His words stung, probably far more than he intended. "As Mother so often reminds me." Elice set the bowl down harder than she meant to and moved toward the door.

"Elice," her grandfather said sharply.

She paused. He was rarely ever cross with her. "Sorry, Grandfather. It's not you I'm angry with."

After a long moment of silence, he said, "Your mother was one of the most empathetic, kind people I have ever known. But becoming a Winter Queen changed her. Her emotions are locked behind a barrier of ice. Still, she fights to be the human she isn't. Doesn't that say enough about her character?"

Elice had heard that excuse too many times. And it was not completely true. There had been a time when her mother was happy, like the light that filtered through Elice's prisms, fractured but full of color. But that had been before . . .

Elice kept her back to her grandfather so he wouldn't see the anger building up inside her until she felt she might burst.

When she didn't answer, he sighed. "You best hurry along."

"Aren't you coming?" she asked as she started toward the door.

"I'm too old to sit in those thrones, and your mother knows it," he said. "But come to my rooms after. I still have my gift to give you."

"You're going to make me endure this by myself?"

He groaned in frustration, and Elice knew she'd won. "You go ahead. I'll be along," he said.

Relieved, she bypassed the fancy, silver and white dining hall and the library, where she hesitated, casting a longing look at the crates packed with straw and books. She could practically feel the velvety texture of the vellum, the whirls and edges the pen had left, dancing under her fingertips. She wondered if Adar liked to read, if she should bring him some books to keep him occupied while his shoulder healed. She might even let him look at her atlas when she was done with it.

With a sigh, she forced herself to keep going, trudging through the white halls with wide ice windows, stray bits of sunlight catching the fine layer of frost in a dazzling display of sparkle. At the palace foyer, her feet crossed the elice blossom—her namesake—that her mother had asked her to shape in the floor using different colors of ice—white, clear, black, blue, and gray.

To Elice's left, the throne room doors were already closed. She had the sense of being watched before she heard the low, growling voice of a wolf fairy—Lowl, whom Elice hated almost as much as she hated the Summer Queen. Elice nearly turned around; surely the rabbit fairy would repeat the story to her later. But Elice's mother would be angry if she didn't show up. Perhaps angry enough to send a fairy to her cave to find her and instead discover Adar. And Elice had promised Chriel.

Bracing herself, Elice grabbed both handles of the massive door and pulled with all her strength. She managed to crack it open just enough to peek into the second-floor balcony. She was very late. But unfortunately not late enough to have missed Lowl's summary of the war. Wearing a pelt dress, the fairy was pacing back and forth through the air before the balcony, her tail low and her head down as if stalking prey. Her yellow fangs were bared as she recounted stories of the summer fairies' laziness and deceit, stirring up the other fairies' hatred for next winter.

Elice's gaze fell to the four chairs directly before her. Her mother sat in one, her right elbow crooked on the armrest of her throne, and a blood-red apple held delicately in her hands. Her mother loved apples above all else and always brought a bounty back from summer, even though the apple trees were barely in bloom—some kind of deal she'd made with an apple fairy.

One chair was for Elice. The other two sat empty. One for her grandfather. The other chair . . . Elice stared at it, suddenly overcome with longing to be a little girl again, giggling as she barreled into her father's arms. The thrill of being tossed into the air, hanging suspended for a moment with the whole world spread in front of her before she fell back into the safety of his arms.

Her eyes went unfocused. Her father would never sit on his throne again. And with his death went the last of Ilyenna's humanity. The Winter Queen had blamed Nelay, the Summer Queen, for luring her away for peace talks. She lived for one thing now—killing Nelay or making her suffer the same fate.

A hand at Elice's back made her start and turn around. With one eyebrow cocked in amusement, her grandfather motioned for her to enter the room. He wasn't going to make her go alone. She shot him a relieved smile that quickly faded when she noticed the silence emanating from the throne room.

That could only mean she'd been spotted.

Taking a deep breath, Elice stepped through the doorway. Beyond the balcony, the room was enormous—three stories tall and just as wide. The far side was open to the air, offering the fairies, who hated enclosed spaces, a feeling of openness. Beyond the columns was a view from the east side of the palace, white ice floating on the black surface of the ocean.

From floor to ceiling and wall to wall, the throne room was packed with fairies. And all of their small, pitiless eyes were on Elice. Lowl bowed stiffly, obviously furious with the interruption. The rest of the fairies followed suit. Elice forced her head high as she braved the silence and walked forward to sit in the chair beside her mother, who didn't acknowledge her at all. Her grandfather sat in the chair next to Elice's and folded his hands calmly in his lap.

As soon as the two latecomers were seated, Lowl launched back into her speech. "It's true, the borders of the Winter Queendom are retracting, as they do every year, but we are making the Summer Queen fight for every mountain, every stream she claims for the Summer Realm. At summer's end, we will be ready to take back what's ours. And this time, we will set a trap that Nelay and her spoiled band of summer fairies will never escape!"

The fairies behind Lowl erupted in a chorus of hissing and growling. The tinny, high-pitched sound from the cold fairies that made Elice's ears ache.

Her mother leaned toward her, the hand with the apple falling to her lap. "You're late, Elice," she whispered. "I expected you to come straight from the forest."

Elice sighed. "I had to get dressed."

"You should have been dressed this morning."

"I found a fox this morning. He was badly hurt. I've been looking after him."

Her mother sat straight on her throne again. "Everything has its end, Elice. It is not something to be feared. Just a natural part of the Balance."

"You were a healer once. You taught me everything I know," Elice said, remembering the hours she used to spend with her mother. But that was before her father died, not long after the War of the Queens had begun.

Her mother made a sound low in her throat. "Perhaps I did." She returned her attention to Lowl and held out a hand to stop the fairies' commotion. "Thank you, Commander. For the battles fought and won. We nearly had Nelay twice due to your cunning."

Lowl bowed low, her yellow eyes flashing with pleasure at the compliment.

"Keeper of the histories, come forward," Elice's mother's voice rang out like tinkling glass.

The fairies pulled back, creating an empty space around Chriel as she flew forward. She wore the mantle of the keeper of the histories—a cloak of white feathers with the black striations of a snow owl.

Elice shot her a proud smile, but the fairy didn't look her way. A little disappointed, Elice slumped in her seat. Most of the fairies were cunning and cruel. There was no humanity about them. No kindness or gentleness. They were nature incarnate. But Chriel was different . . . most of the time.

Behind the rabbit fairy, the snow fairies called for small flakes, which danced and spun on the air currents created by the wind fairies. Elice leaned forward eagerly, wondering which story Chriel would tell. In the past, they'd heard the stories of the gruesome end of one Winter Queen, along with the rise of another. Sometimes there were stories of courage and love and loss from their former lives. Sometimes a key battle between winter and summer was recounted, with winter always ending up the winner.

"Since the beginning," Chriel began, "the world has needed magic to survive. Since the beginning, magic has been ruled by the Balance. And since *our* beginning, we fairies have risen and fallen with the rise and fall of our animals, plants, or elements." Behind Chriel, the wind and snow formed a frozen landscape that slowly began to melt, the tundra coming to life. A field of cotton grass grew, the wooly heads shifting in the breeze. They became smaller as the view widened, revealing two muskoxen charging each other. Their heads met in an explosion that rocked the world around them. Surrounding the muskoxen were fairies making the plants grow and change. Giving the animals their instincts.

"But we were not *the* beginning," Chriel went on. Now the field of cotton grass and muskoxen blurred, until no shapes at all were discernible in the shifting snow. "I was born at the death of the Second Age. Though I was little more than a kitten, I remember . . .

"Magic was different then—it was held by the many creatures of the earth, but mostly by the races of man—elves and dwarves, and even Hebocks, who wielded it for good or evil." Each creature was formed in the snow. The elves had pointed ears and an unearthly beauty. The dwarves were squat, solid, and covered in frizzy hair. The Hebocks resembled a cross between a gorilla and a human.

Chriel stared at the images, but her gaze was distant, as if she were seeing what she described in her memories instead of in front of her. "And I saw these creatures of the Second Age use their magic against each other. I saw their wars. I saw their corruption." A long column of elves wound through a dense wood. They wore beautiful, flowing robes. One of them held a child in her arms, and the child fussed and cried while the elven mother tried to comfort it.

Then men poured from the covers of trees. Hundreds of them. And though the elves fought with a quiet desperation and breathtaking skill, they were vastly outnumbered. Holding the child tight in her arms, the elven woman fled.

The images faded away to become snow once more. "The Balance dictates that all things—even magic—must eventually die and then experience a rebirth," Chriel said darkly. A woman was formed. Large with child, she ran through the clashing armies, hands protectively over her stomach.

"And like a woman in travail, the Balance labors to beget the magic anew. What those of the Second Age did not realize, what they did not understand, was that the Balance is weak at this time—vulnerable. And like a birth, if the new magic is twisted against the Balance, it can destroy both. This is called the Sundering." More battles were fought in the silent swirl of flakes. A Hebock tore a man in half and roared soundlessly. Giants the size of icebergs ripped ancient trees from the ground and swung them at the armies. Hidden between two of these dead giants, the woman screamed as her pains overtook her.

"The Sundering could not be diverted, and so the magic chose one to restore Balance, lest the whole world be destroyed." Elice saw a new woman, beautiful with delicate features, pull back the string of a bow with deadly efficiency as she rode a horse through a battlefield. But Elice's eyes caught on the black horse, for it was much larger and perfectly formed than the other horses around it. A spiral horn sprouted from its magnificent head. This must be a unicorn.

"Her name was Ara, and she was chosen to save those she could from the Sundering. It was she who selected the boundaries of the new magic—that it would be wielded by elemental beings led by dispassionate women. That form became the fairies of winter and summer, led by immortal queens who lived their lives separate from the influence of men."

The battle was over. The woman had brought forth her child. The wind stopped, the flakes drifting without direction, and Elice's gaze shifted to Chriel. "Though this age has passed from memory, I watched as the races of elves and men merged into one. I saw the Hebocks die out. Watched the giants turn to the stone we now call mountains. And I pass my knowledge on so that we might never forget." Chriel dropped her head, her wings trembling.

Elice had heard some of these stories before, in a book of fables Chriel had given her not long ago. But something was wrong. First, Chriel had seemed sad, and if Elice didn't know better, she now seemed frightened.

Ilyenna tapped a finger impatiently on her throne's armrest. "Thank you for this *story*, Chriel." She took a breath to begin the next part of the ceremony.

Chriel raised her head. "I'm not finished, my queen. I have not come this day to simply recite the histories, but also to deliver a warning."

Elice made a choking sound. No one dared challenge the queen, especially not before the entire assemblage of fairies.

Ilyenna rolled her apple between her hands, her gaze narrowed in a warning that Chriel didn't see as she turned in a slow circle to face the fairies around her. "The time has come again. The Fairy Age is ending. The magic is dying." The fairies went very still, only their wings betraying their movement.

The rich red of the apple in Ilyenna's hands was suddenly lost beneath a layer of frost. Slowly she set it down on the table. "Have you too fallen for the Summer Queen's lies, Chriel?" Ilyenna's voice was full of regret.

If any other fairy had said these words, she would have been banished to summer, where she would be sick and lost until Nelay found and killed her. Ilyenna was giving Chriel a chance to take it back, whether because she had been the first fairy to choose Ilyenna as queen, or because of her years of tutelage to her daughter, Elice wasn't sure. She only knew Chriel had to take it back. Pronounce these stories just that—stories best left to dusty books of legends.

Elice's eyes begged the fairy to back down, but Chriel refused to meet her pleading gaze. "I have never been against you, my queen," said the rabbit fairy. "I chose you because I sensed you were important to easing us through the rebirth."

"Don't force me to make an example out of you, Chriel." Ilyenna's voice was like the quiet before the blizzard.

Elice held her breath, silently begging Chriel not to push her mother. But Chriel simply tipped her head to the side and said, "Can you not all see the truth? The tremors that shake the mountains flat, the explosions of fire and ash that bring them up again. Already, dozens of varieties of plants, animals, and insects have died out completely, never to be seen again." When the last of their animals had died, so had the fairies.

Streams of shimmering cold spread out from Ilyenna, but still Chriel went on. "Each rebirth is different. The Unicorn Age would have ended with the races destroying themselves, and perhaps the Balance with it. The Fairy Age will end in explosions of fire and ash and the quaking of the earth."

Everywhere Ilyenna's skin touched, hoarfrost spread, coating her throne in thousands of needlelike spears. "All of which are brought about by the Summer Queen to substantiate her lies."

Chriel sighed. "Only the lands between—the lands fought over by both queens, the lands where summer and winter clash— are affected. How do you explain that?"

It grew so cold that frost formed in the air, sparkling as it drifted. "You were one of my most powerful, trusted fairies. How far you have fallen," the Winter Queen said, sounding tired.

"Chriel, don't!" Elice warned softly.

Ignoring her, Chriel clenched her clawed hands. "You might still stop it, Ilyenna. Make peace with summer. Right the Balance, else the Sundering destroy us all."

Ilyenna rose, and even Elice shrank away from the cold radiating from her like daggers. "I will never make peace with the Summer Queen!"

Elice knew Chriel, knew that determined set to her wings. She was nothing if not a master teacher. And she wouldn't stop until the lesson was understood. "So be it, Ilyenna, Queen of Winter. You seal your own doom, and the doom of us all."

"Mother, please," Elice begged. "She's upset—"

Ilyenna held out a hand to silence Elice. "Chriel, have you been filling my daughter's head with these lies?"

Elice shot Chriel a pleading look. But instead of backing down, the rabbit fairy flew forward. "They are not lies."

"Traitor!" Ilyenna cried, a ball of icy light forming on her palm. Elice shot from her chair, diving for her mother. But her grandfather grabbed the collar of her tunic, which cut into her neck and threw her balance off. Choking, she fell back into her chair.

"Ilyenna," Otec said, his voice strained.

She turned to regard her father for half a moment. Then her gaze fell on her daughter.

"Please," Elice gasped.

"An example must be made," Ilyenna said.

"Please!" Elice cried out. "Not her. Anything but her."

For once, Ilyenna's expression softened. The brilliant silver light faded. She faced Chriel and threw her hand out. A band of ice entrapped the fairy, pinning her wings to her body. Chriel plummeted to the floor, landing with a light thud. "Take her to the dungeons. I'll decide what to do with her later."

A fairy shifted into a raptor, swooped down, and grasped Chriel's shoulders in its wicked talons. She cried out, purple blood leaking from the piercing wounds. Elice wanted to beg them to be gentle, yet she knew she was lucky Chriel had not been banished to the summer realm. Elice dared not push her luck. "Thank you, Mother," she breathed.

Ilyenna eased onto her throne. "I have not yet decided Chriel's fate. She may still die."

Elice leaned toward her mother, her hand raised imploringly, but her grandfather took hold of her arm in a remarkably firm grasp. "I'll talk to her. Later. You go."

"Grandfather," Elice whispered, "Chriel is the only friend I have."

He looked at Ilyenna over her shoulder. "I'll do what I can."

Elice hesitated. If anyone could get through to her mother, it was her grandfather. She listened to him, sometimes.

She was about to go when her mother held out the frost-covered apple. "It's ruined now, and I can only bargain for so many. I suppose you want it for your collection?"

Elice stared at the apple, which was frozen, just like her mother's heart. Biting the inside of her cheek to keep from saying something that might make things worse, Elice took the apple and regally rose to her feet so the fairies wouldn't see her weakness. She pivoted and left the throne room as fast as she dared, knowing thousands of eyes watched her every move.

5

oments before Adar heard footsteps pounding down the stairs hidden behind the tree, the seal alerted him that someone was coming. Adar grabbed a rock and hid it behind his back in case he had to defend himself. Elly pushed open the door and seemed surprised to find him staring back at her. Her face was red as if she'd been crying. Her arms tightened around the clothing she was carrying, practically strangling them. "What are you doing here?" she said sharply.

He raised a single eyebrow as he discreetly tucked the rock under the sealskin beneath him. "You dragged me to your cave and demanded I stay, remember?"

Elly glared at him, a line forming between her furrowed brows. "Don't you know it's death to anyone who approaches the Winter Palace?"

Adar stared at the warm-looking clothing in her arms. "There are more important concerns at present. First, it's freezing in here. And you ripped off all my clothes earlier and fed them to the sea."

Growling, she set a cup of something on the table and shoved the clothing at him. The movement jostled his shoulder, but he kept the pain from showing in his features. The cloth was thick wool, thank the Balance. He let the rug drop from his shoulders, shivered hard, and shook out the tunic, struggling to find the hem. The girl huffed in exasperation and pulled it over his head, scraping against the lump on his head. This time Adar couldn't hold in a grimace, but luckily the tunic covered his face. He pushed his good arm through its sleeve, but let the other sleeve dangle empty.

He tried to pull on the trousers, but bending at the waist re-kindled the fierce burn in his shoulder. "Elly, I would prefer a quick death by drowning instead of freezing to death in this cave." It was the closest he could come to asking for help.

With eyes full of distrust she stared at the trousers and his bare legs. "You're so . . . hairy."

"Well, they won't give you slivers," he said in exasperation. Still, she didn't move. "You went through a lot of work to save me only to let me freeze to death now." This time, he couldn't keep the chatter from his voice.

Still looking wary, Elly knelt down and held them open for him. When he rested his palm on her back, she winced like *he* was hurting *her*. Finally, he had the trousers on. They were too short and far too wide, as was the shirt. Adar would complain later. Right now, he was too grateful for their warmth.

He smoothed his hair and made sure the cord that tied it back was still in place. "I admit, though many a woman has helped me out of my clothes, not one has ever helped me back into them."

Elly shot him a disgusted look. "Where did you get all those scars?"

"An accident when I was younger. I would have died, but my mother saved me."

"Why are you here?"

"We were lost in a storm, we and another ship. With the clouds covering the stars, we were sailing blind. We didn't realize how far off course we were until we saw the sky this morning. Then the winter fairies came and sank our ship."

Elly helped him put on some heavy boots that were too big. "Who is 'we'? Are you Svass?"

Adar considered lying, then decided he probably couldn't pull it off. "I'm a tribesman from the Adrack Desert."

She jerked back. "The tribesmen are in league with the Raiders! The Summer Queen's consort is a tribesman! You even speak the same language—Idaran."

Adar cocked an unconcerned eyebrow. "We're not in league with the Idarans. We simply peacefully coexist with them. Just as we do with the clansmen to the north. It was our language before it was theirs."

Elly didn't seem convinced. "Why would tribesmen come so far north?"

He longingly eyed the cloak in her hands. "Blubber. We need to light our lamps just as much as the next nation, and the Svass are charging exorbitantly high fees for blubber of late."

"What of the girl you were speaking of? The one you were so desperate to find."

He chuckled at the irony. "I haven't found her yet, but I will."

"You mean she wasn't on the ship?"

Exactly what had he been muttering? Not wanting to trap himself in a lie, Adar said simply, "No." He gestured to the fancy cloak. She hesitated then handed it to him. He eagerly wrapped it around his shoulders. Dressed in an ill-fitting ensemble fit for royalty, he knew he looked utterly ridiculous.

"Whose clothes are these?"

Elly started feeding strips of meat to the pup. "My grandfather's. He never wears his ceremonial clothes, so they're least likely to be missed."

Complain later, Adar told himself as he pushed himself to his feet. Only years of training let him keep his balance. He looked down at her as she nervously shifted her weight from one foot to another. She was perhaps the most easily read person he'd ever met.

"Just remember, I can kill you any time I want," she declared.

It hurt to laugh. Adar almost didn't mind the pain. "Your queen already tried."

Elly looked away. "Your lunch is on the table."

Food. It was his one true love. He walked over to the table, looked down, and nearly choked on his saliva. "Blood? You brought me a cup of blood?"

"Cooking the meat makes it weak. We eat it raw."

Imagining the rich foods of his homeland, Adar muttered under his breath, held the cup to his lips, and gulped it down. Then he slammed the cup onto the table and wiped at the blood leaking down the sides of his cheeks. "Tastes like metal." He scrubbed his tongue on the roof of his mouth. "Where's the rest of my lunch?"

"In the kitchens, where it belongs. You can't eat meat yet."

Adar held up an indignant finger. "How come the seal gets meat?"

"Because Picca isn't freshly injured."

He looked the seal over. "She doesn't look injured at all."

Elly winced. "I want her to put on more weight before I release her."

Adar wasn't sure if she was trying to convince him or herself. She was obviously attached to the creature. He worked his tongue, trying to get the taste out. "Whose blood is that anyway—a sacrificial virgin?"

Elly gave him an exasperated look. "It's seal blood."

He glanced at the animal she was feeding. "So the seal is a cannibal?"

"It's only fair. After all, Picca's mother was trying to eat her."

Fire and burning, what kind of hell had he stepped into? "Do seals normally eat their young?"

Elly shook her head. "They're starving." Done feeding the seal, she settled down in the cage. The creature immediately scooted onto her lap, and Adar swore it started purring. "We need to talk about how we're going to get you out of here," Elly told him.

He shrugged and then really wished he hadn't. "Easy, we'll find the other ship and sneak out under cover of darkness."

She looked at him as if he were daft. "Dark? Once the sun rises in the Winter Queendom, it circles the horizon for months before disappearing again."

Adar passed a hand over his face. "This whole place is unnatural."

Elly crossed her arms and huffed. She was cute when she was irritated. "First things first," Adar said. "I'm guessing you have a lookout tower somewhere in this palace. Get me up there, and I'll see if I can find the other ship." He headed for the secret door.

Elly extricated herself from the seal pup and started coming after Adar. "If the Winter Queen or one of her fairies sees you—"

He studied the ice tree, trying to figure out how it opened. "You wouldn't let that happen. After all, you'd be in almost as much trouble as I would if they found you harboring me." He hoped. "You need me gone almost as much as I need to leave." Plus, he had to investigate the layout of the palace. His mission might still be salvageable.

She stepped up beside him and pressed her full lips into a thin line—an unfortunate use of them. "You need to rest. You're badly injured."

Not like I could forget, what with the burning in my shoulder and the pounding in my head. Adar found the handle disguised as a bough and pulled. The door swung silently inward. "I'm a fast healer."

Elly jammed her foot into the base of the door. "How do I know I can trust you?"

He shot her a look over his shoulder. "Really, Elly, I just want to go home. I'm unarmed in a place where everyone has magic and the air alone could kill me in a couple minutes. What could I possibly do to you, or anyone else for that matter?" Technically, he could do a lot of things, but she didn't need to know that.

"You're going to get us both caught."

He rubbed his forehead, letting some of his emotion bleed through. "Those sailors who died—they were my friends. The men in the other ship are my friends too. I have to warn them."

She stared at him, her expression conflicted before pity took over and she stepped back.

He started up the stairs, looking around appreciatively at her handiwork. "Tell me, Elly, if you're the queen's ward, why do you live in a cave and why were you dressed like a servant this morning?"

She hurried after him. "I don't live in a cave. And those were my old clothes."

He grunted, not quite believing her. Now they stood before another door. Adar reached for the handle, but she stepped around and blocked him, saying, "You're risking my life as well as your own. We do this my way or—"

He frowned at her. "Are all wards as demanding as you?" She took a breath as if preparing to berate him, but he neatly sidestepped her and pulled the door open.

"You can't just—" she began, but he held out his hand to silence her.

"This is amazing," Adar said in awe.

His breath left his body in a puff of white, and he momentarily forgot the constant pain in his shoulder. He turned a slow circle. He'd expected a palace made of ice—but not this intricacy, this attention to detail. Nor the colors, for though the sculptures were of ice and snow, they were also prisms that caught the weak sunlight, scattering bursts of color throughout the room. There were sculptures of animals, flowers—everything to be found in nature. All made of prismatic shapes. There was even a long table of vases filled with frozen flowers, and strangely enough, a frozen apple.

He turned a slow circle, trying to take in everything at once. But it was the carved relief in one corner that caught his eyes. A dozen geometric shapes, arranged in a circle. In the center was Elly, her face breaking apart in a kaleidoscope of eyes and lips. It was like she was watching, waiting. Always waiting. Wanting to speak but unable to.

Loneliness lurked in her eyes. Adar reached out to brush his fingertips across the flat planes of the carving. He turned to face the girl who'd pulled him out of the ocean. Her thick dark hair and pale skin fit in perfectly with the cold surrounding her. But not her eyes. They were the color of a pine forest at dusk— blacks and browns with hints of emerald beneath.

"Are these the princess's rooms?" he asked. Who else could make such marvelous things?

Elly huffed. "The princess didn't make it, I did. And these aren't her rooms—they're mine." She turned away. "The princess can form ice that's malleable for a few hours. I shape it."

Adar ran his fingers over the cold branches. "How did you get the proportions so perfect?"

She nodded to one of a dozen shelves of books tucked away between tree and wall. He went eagerly to the books and pulled one down. It was heavy. He set it on a small round table, undid the clasp, and let the pages come open. He reveled in the familiar velvety feel of the vellum. There were drawings of trees in the sides of the pages, the branches twining into clannish knots, the writing a beautiful calligraphy. And while the drawings were beautiful, it didn't convey the depth, textures, or proportions of a real forest—all of which Elly had managed to skillfully capture. "You didn't get this from a book."

She pulled the book from his hands with more than a little possessiveness, shut and clasped it, and lovingly placed it back on the shelf. "I have dreams sometimes, of a place that looks like this. Mountains capped in white. Dark-green trees and bright-gold fields. Stone houses with wooden roofs. There is so much color and light—no matter how hard I try I can never get enough of either."

Adar realized he couldn't read her this time. Something wasn't right. Elly was lying to him or hiding something. He wasn't sure which. "Why the cave, when you have an extravagant room like this?"

She narrowed her gaze. "The palace is made of ice. A fire would melt it. I have to dry my hair somehow after I go swimming. And I need a place to heal the animals."

"Swimming?" he said in disbelief. "You go swimming out there?"

"How do you think I saved you?" she retorted. It was a good point. Not that he'd admit it. "The queen changed me with a kiss," Elly continued. "I wouldn't survive here without it."

He picked up the frozen apple, thinking it didn't quite fit in with the frozen-flower motif. At her dark expression, he set it back down. He had more pressing concerns, and this pretty ward wasn't one of them. "You're not what I expected."

She folded her arms, shifting from one foot to another. Nervous again. "What did you expect?"

Not this yearning, not this eye for loneliness. Adar smiled at her. "I didn't expect such beauty." Might as well flirt with her—after all, she was growing prettier by the minute. And he needed something to do until he found the princess.

Elly pressed a hand to her chest. "You think it's beautiful."

He was confused a moment before he realized she thought he meant her art. "I meant you, but the sculptures are nice too." She blushed and he had to suppress a smile—this mission might be more fun than he'd thought. "Show me this tower," he said.

"No. I'll go look. You head back to the cave."

Adar backed toward the door, hand up. "You've forced this upon me, you know. I'll have to wander the palace, lost and vulnerable. I just hope I don't get caught."

Rolling her eyes, Elly marched past him. "I should have left you to drown," she muttered under her breath, then opened the door a sliver. He stepped behind her as she peered up and down the corridor. This close, he could smell her—the fresh, cool scent of an oncoming snowstorm. She turned and tugged his hood up farther over his face, her hand brushing his temple. "I don't see anyone. Keep your hood up, just in case. From a distance, any fairy who sees you will assume you're my grandfather."

Adar crooked a smile at her, the one that had always worked for him before. Her brow crinkled in confusion and she stepped into a wide corridor. Brushing off her reaction, or lack thereof, he glanced around. This was more what he'd been expecting— white with shades of gray and cool blue. It was intricate, with delicate, lacy arches. There were tables with frozen splays of ice flowers, all of them in the angled shape Elly seemed to prefer.

"You made these?" he asked in surprise.

She turned back to him, holding a finger to her full lips. "I made all of it—the entire palace. I add to it every year."

He followed her, trying to stop gawking and pay attention to his surroundings for when the time came to make his escape. "And what does your princess do while you're making pretty things?"

From ahead of him, Elly's shoulders stiffened. "Doing her mother's wishes, as a good little princess does."

No denying the bitterness in her tone. Perhaps she resented her princess. Adar tucked that information away for future retrieval. They wound their way up a high tower, the stairs made of a densely packed snow that somehow retained its traction.

Elly stepped up through the floor, peering about carefully before looking down at him. "You'll be on display for any fairy to spot. Perhaps you should wait below."

"I have to see for myself," he whispered. If the second ship had sunk, he was stranded in the queendom, and more than his own life was at stake.

Her mouth tightened. "All right. Just let me check first." She climbed the rest of the way up and stood at the edge, then moved out of his line of sight. He heard her soft steps slowly circling.

He came up to find her looking through a telescope made of ice, the freezing breeze tugging at her long hair as she searched the horizon. "There is nothing. Only the endless sea." Adar sniffed, noting indignantly that she didn't even shiver.

He held out his hand. She placed the telescope in it. The cold sides burned into his already freezing skin. He scanned in all directions, shocked at the perfect clearness of the lens. But he didn't see another ship. How was he going to get out of here without a ship? He handed her the telescope and blew into his cupped hands.

"Will the ship leave without you?" Elly asked.

He considered the men he'd met over the journey. Young and old, rich and poor. They all had one thing in common— pride. But they weren't suicidal, either. "Probably." Especially if they realized the *Drauga* had sunk. Fire and burning, if Adar was going to die, did it have to be in this frozen wasteland? Why not in the midst of a battle, his blood singing through his veins? Or at the side of a beautiful woman.

He glanced sidelong at Elly—maybe that last one was more attainable than he'd imagined. But the wind picked up, cutting through the sealskin cape like it was nothing. He shivered hard, a jolt of pain tearing through his shoulder from the involuntary movement.

She stepped toward him, her fingers hovering over his cheek. "What does it feel like to be cold?" she asked, withdrawing her hand.

Trying to keep the pain from showing in his expression, Adar blinked at her. "Like you're slowly becoming an icicle."

Elly took a step back. "We better get you out of the wind."

She led the way down the steps. Adar was shivering so hard he had to lean against the outside wall with his good shoulder to keep his balance, which slowed him down even more. He needed more of that tincture—he could feel it wearing off fast. And right after that, the heat of the fire. But first things first. "I need heavier clothes."

She paused at the base of the stairs, her bottom lip caught by one of her pearly teeth. She looked him up and down and must have noticed he was starting to struggle from the cold and pain, for her face softened. "There is a chest of clothing that might work."

He waited for her to take him to it, but she only stared at him, something unreadable in her gaze. He let out a long-suffering sigh. "Well," he prompted finally, "I know I'm pretty to look at and all, but lead on."

Silently she started down a flight of stairs. She moved faster than he did, so she soon turned around and waited for him to catch up. "Adar, have you ever heard of the Sundering?"

His foot caught on a stair and he nearly fell. As it was, the misstep jolted his shoulder and made his head pound anew. "You mean the calamity that's destroying the world?"

Elly's face blanched. He hadn't thought it was possible for her to be paler, but there it was. "So you believe it's real?"

He huffed. "I know it's real."

She pivoted without a word and led him to the second floor. There was another long corridor flanked by four doors. They passed the first two—one that led to an opulent room, the other door closed. "Whose rooms are these?"

"This is the queen's floor."

That's enough to make a man quicken his pace, Adar thought, even as he forced himself to remain calm.

Elly paused before the third door, reached for the handle, and then hesitated. He was about to ask her what was wrong when she set her shoulders and pushed it open.

Inside, the air had a stale quality, as if no one came in here often. It was some kind of study, with a desk and chair. Lining the walls were weapons—clannish, judging by the knots hammered into the surface of the axe head and the handle. There were daggers and short swords and even a bow, though the wood looked dry. Adar suspected one pull would snap it in two.

This would be the king's study. Adar considered taking some weapons—he felt naked without his twin swords on his back—but Elly was already skittish. He had a feeling even the slightest sign of aggression would frighten her into betraying him.

"In the chest," she said, not moving from the doorway. He wondered at her pained expression, but he was too cold to focus on it for long. He pulled back the lid of the trunk. It was full of clannish clothing—tunics and over-tunics, loose trousers, and an intricate clan belt. There was also winter clothing—a thick sheepskin coat and trousers. Heavy boots, too. Gloves. And most importantly, "A hat!"

Adar didn't hesitate to drop the nearly worthless cloak and pull the extra clothing directly over the ill-fitting ensemble he already wore. This time Elice didn't try to help him, so it took longer. Last, he put on the hat. It was sheepskin with flaps that covered his ears and tied under his chin, though he couldn't tie the strings with only one hand. He knew he looked ridiculous, but at least his head was covered.

Under all the layers, he felt immediate relief from the biting cold, but he was still frozen to the bone. And the throb in his shoulder was growing fierce. He still needed to find out where the princess was staying, but he knew his body, knew how far and how hard he could push it. And he was at his limit. "I think I need the fire and something to eat," he told Elly. "And tincture. Lots of tincture." He felt a twinge of conscience for putting her at risk like this, but he hadn't eaten since the night before.

She nodded. "Wait here. I'll be back."

"I'd rather come with you," Adar spoke up, realizing that without any sign of a ship to get him out of here, she might decide she'd be better off turning him in.

She was already halfway down the corridor and didn't look back, and he certainly couldn't keep up with her. He needed to rest if he was even going to make it to the cave. "Meat!" he called after her. Then he found a chair in the study and collapsed into it.

Almost immediately, he noticed the eerie silence, so complete that all he could hear was the beating of his heart. It was disconcerting, being alone in an enormous palace that should have been filled with servants and royalty. Instead, only four people lived here. He didn't know how Elly stood it.

When she finally returned, she had a bowl filled with raw meat, frozen as hard as a rock. Would it have been too much for her to cook it? But then Adar remembered the whole fire-and-ice-palace conundrum. He looked at the meat distastefully, hoping the fire in the cave was still burning so he could cook it. "What I wouldn't give for some roasted lamb basted with a mint sauce."

With a huff, Elly whirled and started up the stairs. "In case you hadn't notice, we don't have lambs. Or mint. Or fire, for that matter."

He rolled his eyes before hurrying after her. "You can't tell me that with all your books you haven't heard of real food and longed for it." She didn't answer. "Oh, come on. There's got to be something you want to eat besides raw meat all the time."

Her steps slowed a little. "I've always wanted to try lamb stew with some of my grandmother's soft bread. And a bowl of raspberries and cream."

Adar felt sorry for her then, that she had never tasted something so simple even the peasants could enjoy it. He followed her up the stairs to the third floor, which was noticeably smaller than the second. Before they stepped into the corridor, he looked around the corner, pretending to be suddenly worried they might be caught. "Does the princess sleep on this floor, too?"

Elly shot him a suspicious glare. "Why are you so interested in her?"

He considered for a moment before deciding he couldn't risk it. "Just don't want to turn into one of your ice sculptures."

She quirked an eyebrow. "But you're not worried about the queen?"

"I thought the queen was busy today."

Elly stepped into her intricate room. Adar noted the hidden lever she used to open the secret door. She gestured for him to enter the room. Obviously she wasn't going to answer him. Very well. There were other ways to find out what he needed to know.

"You're not coming?" he asked warily, wondering if he'd revealed too much.

Her jaw tightened. "They'll be eating dinner soon. You saw where the tincture was." She motioned for him to go down.

Adar hesitated, feeling more than a little guilty for using her. "Thank you. For saving my life. For helping me."

She blinked at him in surprise. Then her mouth turned into a tentative smile, revealing an off-center dimple on her left cheek. "You're welcome."

6

The next morning, Elice squared herself before entering the library. Her grandfather was lying on the sealskin sofa, his legs propped up on pillows as he snored softly. He'd started taking several naps throughout the day. She had tried to give him tincture after tincture, but he'd only waved her off and said there wasn't a remedy for getting old.

Green apple in hand, her mother stood by the huge windows that overlooked the sea, the long, lean lines of her body emphasized by the low-slung clan belt. In that moment, Elice thought her mother was a woman of white, her white dress and white skin reflecting the white light from the snow outside. Surely her blood was white too. For nothing so staining as red pumped through her veins.

Elice rested the tray of their breakfast on the table. Adar hadn't been too far off when he'd thought her a servant. There wasn't much cleaning to do—after all, there wasn't really any dirt in the queendom—but she hunted and prepared their food. And looked after her grandfather. Folding her hands in front of her, Elice waited for her mother to acknowledge her, but the queen didn't bother turning around. "Thank you for sparing Chriel," Elice finally said.

"I'm still not sure I am sparing her."

Elice gasped. "But surely—"

Her mother's long fingers curled around the apple, her nails biting into the flesh. "Chriel openly defied me, and worse still, she undermined my authority. I must send a message to the rest of the fairies."

Elice stepped around the table, coming up behind her mother. "They obey you, Mother, completely and without question." The Winter Queen was one with the fairies—they shared emotions. How could they possibly betray her?

"All winter, there have been whispers of the Sundering among them." Ilyenna's voice was barely above a whisper. "Though I have forbidden it."

Elice stared at the back of her mother's head. "Will you kill everyone who disagrees with you, Mother? Will you kill me?"

Ilyenna turned around. Frost lined her long lashes and the tips of her hair. "Has Chriel turned you against me too?"

"You do that well enough on your own," Elice said through gritted teeth.

The Winter Queen raised an eyebrow. "You forget, Daughter. You are under my protection, afforded all the comforts and diversions I can offer. While I wage war to keep you safe. To keep *us* safe."

Elice shook her head bitterly. "Don't blame this war on me. You're avenging your brother and my father—" She choked on the last word, unable to carry on.

A blizzard stormed behind her mother's eyes. But before either of them could say any more, Elice's grandfather pushed himself to a sitting position and swung his legs heavily off the couch. "Stop bickering, both of you. We are a family—there's nothing more important than that." He pointed a finger at Elice. "Stop baiting your mother." Then he pointed to his daughter, his face softening. "There's nothing wrong with showing mercy, Ilyenna."

Elice's mother brushed the frost from her lashes. "If I show her mercy, I look weak to those who oppose me." She made a slashing motion with her arm. "Any sign of weakness—any— and they could orchestrate my death as they did Leto's." The previous Summer Queen. The two had been friends once.

"Mother," Elice said as gently as she could. There was still light somewhere inside her mother—there had to be. "Let Chriel publicly apologize and show her support for you. Surely that will weaken your enemies while showing that you can still be merciful."

Ilyenna looked away, her jaw tight.

"I agree," Otec said.

"Please." Elice allowed her desperation to bleed into her voice. "Let this be my gift for the rest of the celebration. You don't need to get me anything else."

Ilyenna took a deep breath and let it out. "Fine. If Chriel will agree to publicly apologize and seal her support for me, I will allow her to live."

Elice sagged in relief and covered her mouth with her hand to hide her smile. "Oh, thank you, thank you!" Before she could change her mind, she wrapped her arms around her mother.

Her mother stiffened before awkwardly patting Elice's back. Elice didn't even feel the usual sting of rejection. She whirled around, danced over to her grandfather, and planted a kiss on his sagging cheek. He grunted and mumbled something about not even being allowed to take a nap.

They sat down at the circular table. Elice ate quickly. Her grandfather asked Ilyenna for updates on the clanlands, about the people and family he'd left behind when he'd come to the queendom to help raise Elice after her father's death.

Elice listened to the stories of people she'd never met, but felt she knew all the same. They were her family—cousins from both sides of the family. Even her paternal grandmother was still alive. Though Narium was well into her eighties and practically blind, she still supervised her clan, the Argons, with a firm hand.

Elice longed to meet them, to feel the grass of the Shyle beneath her feet, to know what it was like to whisper secrets into the ears of her female cousins or kiss a boy for the first time. She forced the longing away, determined to enjoy a rare moment of having her family together, sharing a meal of meat and blood.

When they were finished, her grandfather reminded Elice that her gifts from the first day of Winter's End were in his room. They exchanged gifts for the second day, books and carvings and sculptures. Her mother gave her the long-awaited atlas, drawn by a man named Defendi. Elice flipped through the pages, memorizing the names of cities and towns. She was even surprised to see a rough representation of Svass, with the Winter Queendom nothing more than an impassable border with nothing beyond.

Wanting to tell Chriel the good news, Elice soon dragged herself away from the atlas, said goodbye to her mother and grandfather, and hustled to the kitchen. She washed the dishes by scouring them out with a blizzard before setting them back on the shelf. Then she wound her way to the back of the palace and down the plain steps that led to the lowest level, one her mother had said was left over from the previous Winter Queen, who had used it as a prison for the fairies who displeased her. Elice and her family used it to store meat, which hung from the ceiling on long chains. She pursed her lips as she wove through dangling, mostly empty chains—she would have to go hunting soon if she was going to have enough meat to feed an extra mouth.

At the back of the cellar, dozens of iron cages still hung from the ceiling, empty save for one. Two wolverine fairies, all sharp claws and teeth, stood guard on either side. They would be rotated out every few hours or risk becoming sick and weak. They growled and tensed to lunge as Elice came closer.

Shoulders pricking with the sensation of being watched, she squared her shoulders, trying not to think of the time she'd seen two wolverine fairies tear into each other, leaving one bloody and twitching. "My mother said I could come," she told the fairies.

They relaxed, but only slightly. Elice tried to pretend they weren't there as she stepped closer, peering into the shadows. Chriel was huddled in the center of the first cage, her arms wrapped around her legs, and her chin tucked into her chest. Fairies hated being trapped or underground—hated it almost as much as they hated smoke.

Elice reached out to stroke Chriel's head. The wolverine fairies snapped their jaws. Snatching her hand back, Elice peered into the cage. "Are you all right, my friend?" The fairy didn't answer. "Chriel," Elice said carefully, "my mother said she will let you go if you apologize in front of everyone, declare your allegiance to your queen, and work to dispel the rumors of the Sundering among the other fairies."

Elice had expected Chriel to be relieved and appreciative, but she didn't move from her position. "Chriel?" she tried again.

"Sometimes you have to see the truth before you will believe it." The rabbit fairy's words came out muffled.

"I don't understand. Mother won't banish you—why doesn't that make you happy?"

Chriel's pink eyes glittered as she finally looked up. "Ilyenna was broken long ago. They all were. That's the mistake Ara made during the last age. Now you have a chance to make it right."

Chriel was still talking about the Sundering. Angry, Elice took a step closer. "Why would you believe the Summer Queen's lies over your own queen? How could you betray her like this?"

"When it is your turn to choose, Elice, remember that when you choose the good, you also choose the evil."

Tears pricked Elice's eyes. "Chriel! You're going to get yourself killed if you keep up like you are."

Chriel's skin shifted, her mouth elongated, and twitching whiskers formed on her cheeks. Fur rustled from her pores, coating her skin, until she stood as a rabbit instead of a fairy. Her pink eyes fluttered shut, and she pointedly turned away from Elice.

Pushing back the tears that burned her eyes, Elice leaned even closer to the cage, buying her a warning growl from the wolverine fairies. "Fine, Chriel. Refuse to talk about this rationally. Just apologize to my mother and stop this nonsense before it's too late." Elice sniffed, then whirled and marched back up the stairs.

On the first floor, she stopped at the library. Her grandfather was snoring on the couch again. Her mother sat at the broad desk, quill in hand. One of her council fairies, Ursella, perched on the edge of a book.

"I need to go hunting," Elice said, aching for a release for the pent up tension inside her.

Her mother looked up from her book. "Your grandfather told me we have enough meat to last a while."

"I have a fox and a seal to feed," Elice explained.

Her mother sighed disapprovingly. "One of my fairies can bring a seal right to the front doors. You can slit its throat and be done with it."

Elice pursed her lips. "That isn't fair. And the meat was to be my gift to you for tomorrow."

Ilyenna sighed again, this time with long-suffering. "I'm going to orchestrate our withdrawal from summer myself. There are still many mountaintops we have strongholds in. Many battles we can still fight." Which meant Elice's mother planned to steal into the Summer Realm with the night. Battles that would leave behind frozen crops and dead animals.

Elice frowned. Her mother had just arrived, and Winter's End had just begun. "How long will you be gone?"

Ilyenna's attention was already elsewhere. "As long as it takes."

She would take the majority of her fairies with her. At least that meant there was less chance of Adar being discovered. Atlas pressed to her chest, Elice made her way to her room. She left the book on her table and hurried down the secret tunnel to the cave beneath, which now smelled strongly of smoke and cooked meat, with an undercurrent of seal dung. Normally, she'd have replaced all the dirty snow in the pup's pen with fresh, but she couldn't do that with Adar watching.

He was asleep, but woke when she stepped inside. She knelt beside him to set a freshly packed bag of snow around his bruised shoulder. She was pleased to see it didn't look any more swollen than the day before.

"Can you move it at all?" she asked him

Adar nodded as she settled his clothing back in place. "Hurts like fire, but I can."

"Well, that means it probably isn't broken. Another week and you can start taking the brace off and moving it around." She set his breakfast on the table and fed the last of the meat to Picca. Then Elice went to the opposite wall, where her bags were. She took down the sled her father had made her so long ago.

Adar was already standing, his eyes heavily lidded from the poppy. "Where are you going?"

He still wore Elice's father's wool clothing from his youth, that odd hat pressed firmly to his head. She could barely look at Adar for the memories. "We need more meat if we're to keep you alive." She continued past him, but he followed her.

Without a word of complaint, he gulped down the blood she'd brought him. "I'll come with you."

She eyed him. "No leaving the cave, remember?"

He shrugged and his face paled. He reached for his injured shoulder and let out a controlled breath. "Elly, Elly, Elly. I thought we were past this. Besides, I peeked out earlier. The fog's so thick I couldn't see two steps in either direction."

She frowned. He grinned. She rolled her eyes. He wiggled his eyebrows.

"You're not making it easy to keep you alive," she said.

"I never do."

"I might kill you myself."

He started to shrug again and then seemed to think better of it. "My mother says the same thing."

Elice considered sealing off the cave with ice to trap him. But since that would reveal her identity, she decided against it. Besides, her mother would have left with Ursella by now. "Keep your hood over your face, just in case," Elice told him. Then she went back and grabbed two harpoons and a couple of her father's skinning knives. They were rusty but serviceable, and besides, she couldn't very well form an ice spear in front of Adar.

She headed out of the cave, keeping to the base of the mountain and her ice forest for cover. Adar stayed close behind her. He was right about the fog—her ice forest was merely a blur of shadowy shapes to her left. The mountain to her right was the only thing that anchored her bearings.

At the sound of the seals wuffing, Adar froze. "Is that a lion? Do you have lions this far north?"

She chuckled. "That's a baby seal calling for its mother."

Adar's brow furrowed. "I've heard seals before. They sound like a dog."

Elice passed a hand down her face. "That's a sea lion. Seals mew, wuff, grunt, chirp, grumble, boom, chuck, and sing. They do not bark."

Another seal wuffed. "Are you sure? Because that sounded an awful lot like a lion's grunting."

"Don't worry, the fairies did something to the forest. Predators don't come inside."

"This will be a great story to tell the women back home," Adar whispered from behind her.

Elice tensed up. "Are all men as annoying as you?"

"No other men compare to me, Elly. Not in bravery or chivalry or—"

"Cockiness?"

"Only because it's true." She could hear his grin in his voice.

"I should have let you drown," she muttered.

"I know. My presence can be overwhelming at times. But like too-bright sunlight, you'll adjust to my brilliance eventually," he said in exaggerated tones before sniggering at his own joke.

She bit back a reply in the hopes the silence would be catching. It worked. For a few seconds, at least.

"So when do I get to meet the princess?" Adar went on. "And does she like her men tall, dark, and handsome?"

"She likes them quiet and decidedly less hairy." Elice started jogging, hoping to leave him behind as she made her way past the forest and the jutting glacier, where her willow tree stood like a sentinel. On the other side was an ice covered-beach. She could smell the colony of seals before she saw them—a mixture of fish and dung.

Crawling, she eased around the rise and peeked over a drift of snow. The fog was thinner here. She could just make out the seal's dark shapes. She chose a young bull—she didn't want to orphan a pup—that was farthest away from the shore.

She was dismayed when Adar huffed up behind her and dropped to her side. "That was fun." He gasped great puffs of white into the air. At least he had the sense to keep his voice down. "But maybe next time wait until a few days after I nearly died to sprint through this frozen wasteland. I almost lost you in the fog."

"That was sort of the idea."

He grinned. "Worried I'd show you up with my one arm? That would be humiliating."

Elice rolled her eyes and pointed to the seal she'd chosen. "I'm going after that one."

"We won't be able to carry that much meat."

Elice shot him a disbelieving look. "Like you can carry any meat with that shoulder injury."

"I only need one good arm." Adar flexed the one that wasn't injured.

She shoved a harpoon into his grasp. "Try not to get yourself killed. They're faster than they look."

He tested the weight of the harpoon like he knew how to use one. Which was unfortunate, because she was sort of looking forward to him making a fool out of himself. "Circle to the left and scare them toward me." She pointed so he could see what she meant. "Try to angle yourself between them and the water so they don't escape."

Without waiting for his response, Elice disappeared in the fog and skirted the group, then came up on the other side. She dropped to her belly and crawled toward the seals. When she was close enough to hear their heavy breathing, she rose up, steady and smooth, and ran at them.

One seal chirped a warning, and the others started scooting for the water. Elice could make out a faint shadow on the other side that had to be Adar, waving his harpoon to startle the animals, who immediately angled away from him toward the water, and Elice.

She was in the midst of them now, as they shot past in a hazy blur. But her eyes remained fixed on the bull she'd chosen, a half dozen steps away. She lifted the harpoon, the heavy weight pulling at her shoulder. She threw it just as the bull reached the edge of a crashing wave. He bellowed in pain and charged her. She sidestepped and bashed his head with her club.

The seal swung back around, mouth gaping. Elice danced back but lost her balance as a wave pulled her feet out from under her. She crashed into the surf, sputtering. The bull seal charged her again. Without a thought, Elice formed an ice spear and braced it against the hard ground. The bull lunged, impaling itself, and choked on its own blood. Adar was on the animal a moment later, his club striking it hard enough to cave in its skull.

Elice pulled the ice spear back into herself, hoping Adar hadn't noticed it, but he stared at her in disbelief. He shook himself, reached down, hauled her to her feet, and then danced back from a wave that soaked him to his thighs. He gasped, his breath fogging the air. "Fire and burning, that's cold!"

She wiped seawater from her eyes and took hold of the harpoon. "Come on, we need to get him on shore before the waves take him out to sea."

Adar grinned at her through his shivers, his body hunched protectively around his shoulder. "I think I just saved your life." He hadn't, but Elice couldn't tell him that. He helped her roll the animal farther up the shore. "Still, you're quite impressive on your own, Elly."

Her cheeks burned. "You better head back to the cave. I don't want to drag your unconscious body again. And your hood has fallen off." She could tell he was struggling with the cold and that his shoulder was bothering him more than he was letting on.

He tugged the hood back over his head. "You sure you can handle it by yourself?"

She met his gaze steadily. "There's not much here I can't handle." Except maybe him. He didn't argue this time but headed off with his arm wrapped tightly around his body. "I brought you enough food to last for the rest of the day," she called to him. "Stay in the cave. I'll see you in the morning." He waved without looking back.

Elice knelt next to the carcass and ran her hand gently down the soft fur. "I'm sorry," she whispered. She wished it wasn't like this, that she didn't have to kill to survive. Perhaps that was why she healed—to balance what she took.

As the wind picked up, thinning the fog, she butchered the bull quickly, before his scent brought in the bears. She took the meat and settled onto the sled. It wasn't long before she caught sight of a distant polar bear running toward her. The animal outweighed her ten to one, and they were fast. It paused, its nose testing the air, its gaze weighing the competition.

But Elice had most of the meat loaded anyway. She quickly laid down a path of hard snow for the runners. She was barely two dozen steps away when the bear started running again. But he was heading for the bones and intestines, not her.

At the ripping and tearing sounds, Elice forced herself to keep her pace even and her senses tuned to the bear, should it turn on her. She let out a breath of relief when she made it past the trees. She bypassed the cave, came around the back entrance of the palace, and hauled the meat into the kitchen. She had to constantly thaw the meat to prevent it from freezing so she could cut it into slabs, after which she hauled it downstairs.

She paused in her work to visit the dungeon to try to talk to Chriel. Elice even offered to line her cage with soft snow or bring her a book to keep her occupied, but the fairy ignored her. Hurt, Elice turned away and did not approach her again.

When she finished with the meat, Elice stretched out the sealskin on pegs, then spread coarse salt across the top. This took a few hours and left her sticky with seawater and blood. She scoured herself with a blizzard as best she could, then delivered some lunch to her grandfather. He was asleep on his bed again.

She'd just left his food on his nightstand and turned to leave when his gruff voice reached out to her. "Matka, is that you?"

"No, Grandfather, it's only me."

He looked disappointed for a moment, then his gaze brightened. "Elly girl, what time is it?"

"Lunchtime."

He sat up, rubbing his face, and swung his feet out of the bed. Elice couldn't help but notice that they were nearly purple.

"Are you cold?"

"Hmm?" Following the direction of her gaze, he waved her words away. "No, no. Just old, and tired from all the excitement yesterday." He pushed himself to his feet, took his cane, and shuffled toward the chest at the foot of his bed.

Elice gestured to the food at his table. "Aren't you going to eat?"

"Bah, later, later. Bring me a chair, will you, Elly? It's time to give you your gift."

She brought a chair and he sat in it, facing the chest. He motioned for her to open it.

Elice grinned. She loved going through her grandfather's trunk. She pulled back the lid to reveal dozens of books he had bound by hand. She pulled them out and reverently set them on the floor. She'd spent many hours going through the drawings inside. Drawings done by her grandmother. Landscapes mostly, some of great deserts interrupted by onion-domed towers, others of rolling forests and great mountains.

Elice's grandfather held out his hands for one drawing—the one that had the faces of his family, brothers and sisters as well as Ilyenna and her brother Bratton as young children. Elice thought she looked like her mother, except her skin was paler and her body of a thicker build. "Keep going," her grandfather encouraged as she eased through the pages one by one.

Finally, Elice had reached the bottom of the chest. Inside was a long braid of black hair, very much like hers, only without the curl. In a box were some carvings in a box—most of animals.

One day, not long after her father had died and her grandfather had come to take his place, Elice had stolen the animals and played with them in her forest room, pretending they were real as she herded them and hunted them and ran from them in terror. And when she'd grown tired and angry that her handsome, playful father had been replaced by a limping old man, she had snapped the stallion's legs.

When her grandfather found her, he spanked her hard enough to bring tears to her eyes. Elice told him she hated him and that she wished he would go home and her father would come back.

Her grandfather had sat down hard on a chair, staring at the stallion's broken legs. "I made this the day my son was born. A gift for him."

He didn't say any more. He didn't need to. Elice knew the story of her uncle—how he had died in the final battle of Idara. For the first time, Elice realized her grandfather had feelings, and that she had hurt them very badly.

"I made you one too, Elice, the day you were born. I'm not sure what happened to it." He had left her then, with carved animals scattered all over her floor. Elice had gently picked up each one and put them all back in the box, just as she had found them. She had never opened her grandfather's trunk again, not without his permission. But the next day, Elice had her own menagerie of animals to play with, still smelling of fresh-cut wood.

Now her grandfather leaned forward and pointed. "Inside the box." Elice opened the lid and he gestured. "That bundle of cloth there."

Reaching past an otter and a chicken, Elice took out the bundle carefully and handed it to him. He settled it in his lap and unwrapped it to reveal an elice blossom, the stem broken off, and half of a beaver carving, cut straight down the center. He reverently ran his fingers over the splintered edge of the beaver before reaching down and handing the flower to Elice. "I made this for your grandmother. She drilled a little hole in it and wore it as a pendant. I took it off her neck the day we buried her. I should have given it to your mother . . . Now, I'm giving it to you."

Elice stared at the worn carving in her hand. She glanced up at her grandfather, but he wasn't looking at her. His fingertips were on the family drawing, tracing his wife's face without actually touching the vellum.

He didn't bother to hide the tears on his cheeks as he turned the page back and paused on the drawing of his sister Holla, with her wide-set eyes that were tipped up at the edges, and her round, flat face. "The beaver I made for Holla before the Raiders took her. I liked to think she had the other half while I kept this one, and in that way, we were always connected.

Elice's gaze caught on the other woman on the opposite page. Elice thought she could see something of her own face in the lines of her cheeks and the curve of the nose. The woman's eyes were full of mischief. Elice pointed. "Storm?"

Her grandfather nodded as he looked at his other sister's face. "I always wondered what she named her baby. If she ever forgave me."

He shut the book sadly, still holding the beaver carving. "That's enough memories for one day. Put the rest back. But keep the blossom to remind you of love and loss. They go hand in hand, like the fibers of a rope. Rope is what you need to climb a cliff. But it better be long enough, else you'll have to jump."

Her grandfather's mind was wandering again. "I can't take this, Grandfather. It's too special."

He reclined on the bed and pulled the covers up, the carving clenched in his right hand. "Special—yes. And when I'm gone, you can take the beaver, too. I'd give it to you now, only I can't bear to part with it. Not yet. Maybe not until I die."

Tears sprang to Elice's eyes. "Die?"

He met her gaze. "What is it you think I'm doing, child?"

They stared at each other a long time. Elice couldn't deny the truth any longer—she'd already denied it for far too long. Her grandfather was ill. And if he died, she would be left alone and in complete darkness for nearly six months of the year.

7

Elice hurried to her cave and opened the door with her hip. Adar sat before the fire, her atlas in his lap. She put down the food, then swung the furs off her shoulder and onto the table. "What are you doing with that?"

He glanced up at her. "This has the most detailed map of Svass I've ever seen. Every other map is just conjecture mixed with lies. But this—"

She yanked it off his lap. "What made you think you had the right to go in my room?"

"You have books. I was bored."

Try as she might, Elice couldn't blame him for that. She would have done the same. "Next time, ask. And you better not get ashes on any of the pages."

"I would never."

For once, he seemed perfectly serious. Mollified, she checked his shoulder and changed out the snow pack. She was glad for the distraction from her worry and hurt over Chriel. "Have you been taking more tincture?"

"Not as much as yesterday," he admitted as Elice handed him his plate. He took it with a steely look on his face. He gulped down his cup of blood in five swallows. He set it down hard, a great shudder running through him. "Gah! Do you drink this every day?" She glared at him. "The blood is great," Adar murmured. "I love the blood. And the raw meat—delicious. I'm just curious, do you happen to have any . . . I don't know . . . fruit?"

Elice decided then and there not to give him the apple she'd pilfered from the kitchen. "Let me check our garden." She went to the seal chirping from her pen and started dropping strips of meat into her mouth.

"Fruit doesn't grow in gardens," Adar muttered as he dug around on the floor beside him and came up with a long bit of blackened bone with a jagged end. "It grows in orchards."

"It does?" Elice said in surprise, her anger melting away as she rubbed Picca's soft fur while discreetly freezing some of the animal's dung so the cave wouldn't smell so bad. Studying her seal, she realized it wouldn't be long before she had to let the animal go. Just like she would have to let Adar go.

She pushed the thought aside. "What about insects? Do their wings make sound like some of the fairies? Or are they silent, like birds?"

Adar burned the bone tip in the coals and then stabbed the meat onto the end and held it over the flames. "Depends. Bees and flies and mosquitoes make a buzzing sound, so maybe the ones with clear wings make sound. Owls are silent." He shivered lightly.

Elice frowned. "What do owls have to do with it?"

He shivered from head to toe this time. "Have you ever had a decrepit, deranged owl creep up on you?" She shook her head. "Then you could never understand."

Sometimes she wondered how hard this man had hit his head. "What does a tree smell like?"

"Uh, I guess that depends on the tree. Some don't smell at all unless they're in bloom. Some only smell if you break the leaves. Most conifers have a strong, spicy scent all the time."

Elice edged closer to him, ignoring the pungent odor com-ing from the meat. "What does a horse feel like—to touch it, I mean? They seem so sleek."

Adar brought the sizzling meat closer and seemed to decide he wasn't done burning it yet, as he placed it back in the flames. "You know, you could see all this for yourself if you helped me escape."

Elice stared in surprise. "Escape?"

He looked at her as if she were daft. "I can't stay here. The queen or one of her fairies will catch me eventually."

"The ship—"

"Is not coming. I'm going to have to strike out across Svass. Find one of their settlements and work my way south until I find a ship."

She shook her head. "You'd never survive. Not alone."

"Which is why you should come with me."

Her mouth came open in surprise. "What?"

He cocked her a grin. "Why not? Surely you don't want to be stuck in this frozen wasteland for the rest of your life. And if your stuffy old princess came with us, she could use her magic to keep us alive."

He was definitely not getting an apple. "She's not stuffy and old."

Adar chuckled lightly. "Prove it." He pulled out the steam-ing meat and blew on it. "Let me ask her myself."

"Ask her? You can't ask her!"

"Why?" he asked lazily, then nibbled the meat.

Elice scrambled to come up with an excuse. "Because she'd turn you in!"

He cocked an eyebrow. "But you're always saying how honorable she is—"

"No." Elice folded her arms across her chest. "I'm saying she does what her mother tells her. She would turn you in with-out a moment's hesitation."

"Maybe you could convince—"

"I said no," Elice said through gritted teeth.

"Fine. But without her, I don't know how the two of us will survive."

"The two of us?"

Adar grinned. She cast a disdainful glance at the meat. "You're ruining it. Cooking it takes all the strength from the blood."

"I can live with that." He brushed his hands together. "Well, then, while the queen's away, the ward must play." He stood and pulled Elice up beside him before heading for the door. "Let's go outside."

Elice hurried after him, a protest on her lips.

Adar stepped out of the cave and stopped, his mind struggling to match what he was seeing with what he knew of the world. Before him was an entire forest made of ice in a dozen different shades of winter. There were crystal-clear trunks with black ice leaves. Clear ice with bubbles and ribbons twisting through trunks like rivers. Leaves made of white ice. Trees of blue-black and sea-green. In the branches was an almost turquoise bird leaning down to feed a beetle to her chicks. But as Adar went farther into the forest, the trees became less and less like real trees and more and more angular.

"This was here yesterday?" he asked Elly.

"The fog hid it. You should come back inside."

He peered up through the icy leaves, searching for the glimmer of sunlight on lithe bodies. The sound of wings. But there was nothing. "Stop worrying, Elly. Fairies never take much notice of humans anyway, not unless they have reason to."

"How do you know so much of fairies, anyway? I was under the impression that the Sight was rare."

He stumbled a little. "Er, my father is something of a historian—he has studied the lore of the fairies and the records of men." Adar reached out to touch the flank of an ice bear's white body, all hard planes and wide angles. "How is this possible?"

Elly didn't look back at him—she was too busy staring at the sky, no doubt looking for fairies. "Every winter, during twilight months, the princess and I add to her ice forest."

He studied her, not quite believing she had created all of this. There was nothing to gain by voicing his suspicions, so he kept them tucked away. "Twilight months?"

She glanced back at him, and he was again amazed by how pale she was—he could see the faint tracing of veins beneath her skin. "One hundred and eighty-seven days when the sun does not set, but instead climbs ever higher on the horizon before falling again. Twenty-four days of twilight. One hundred and sixty-three days of never-ending dark." She shuddered lightly, probably not even realizing she'd done it. But Adar was trained to notice such things.

He couldn't really blame her—he couldn't imagine living nearly six months in total darkness. He turned in a full circle and then headed toward a strange sight. As he came closer, he realized what he was seeing was indeed a tree, or rather, two perfectly flat ones joined in the exact center, almost like they were cut pieces of vellum.

He rested his hand on the side, noting the burning cold even through his sheepskin gloves. "I don't understand."

Elly cleared her throat. "Every spring, the queen brings us books about the world—plants, animals, cultures. Whatever she can find. When I was younger, my adoptive father, Rone, would read them to me. Of course, I knew trees weren't flat, but that's how I always saw them. And that's the way I grew to love them." She rested her hand on the tree, alongside Adar's. "Whenever I look at these trees, I hear his voice. The feel of his body next to mine, his heart beating against my back."

Adar stared at her, admiring the passion. "And where is your father now?"

She dropped her gaze. "He died when I was younger."

He reached out and squeezed her hand. "I'm sorry." Elly nodded and he took a step toward her, snow crunching beneath his feet. "There's something beautiful about how you see the world." Their gazes met, and Adar took in her forest-at-dusk eyes and full bottom lip. He suddenly realized he'd been looking too long. And not just looking, but admiring.

She glanced up at the sky. "Can . . . can I show you something else?"

"Please do."

She tugged off his mitten and took his hand, and he was surprised to realize the wind didn't feel as cold as before. He let her pull him along, her palm cool but not in an unpleasant way. It was strange to intimately touch this girl he barely knew—in fact, he quite liked it. Which was a bad idea. He hadn't come all this way to be distracted from his mission.

She led him to a tree that looked to be made of twisting ribbons forced from the sky to join at the trunk. He touched a flat ribbon of ice. "It's an aurora," Elly said.

"If no one ever sees it, why do you make them?"

Her expression clouded. "What do you give to people who have everything?"

"The queen? You make it for her? Why?"

Elly looked over the ocean, toward the crimson horizon. "To say I'm sorry." Her gaze was haunted and full of longing.

Adar looked back at the magnificent palace, enormous and intricate. This was how she showed her adopted family she loved them. But he got the feeling they didn't appreciate it. "Would you make something for me?" He wanted to take the words back as soon as he'd said them. But with the look of longing on her face, and the way she'd dismissed her art, he wanted her to know it had value.

Elly bit her lip. "Really?"

He couldn't take it back now, not when she looked so unsure. "Please."

Her grin widened. "The princess knows how to tie what I make to winter, so it won't ever melt. I can ask her to help me make you something if you like."

"Surprise me."

Her gaze turned inward even as she tugged him up a sharp rise to where one of her trees stood alone. This one was made of thousands of diamond-shaped prisms. It was beautiful, but not as imaginative as some he'd already seen. When they reached the top, Adar left Elly and the tree behind and moved to the edge of the glacier. He noted a beach of seals to his right. Before him, the horizon stretched on as far as he could see. He squinted, searching for any sign of the other ship. But all he could make out was the flat, oblong shapes of the ice floe interrupted by the occasional iceberg, which the ships would give a wide birth.

He thought of his shipmates. The other ship. He hoped they made it out alive, even though they had left him stranded behind enemy lines.

The sun slipped around some clouds. Adar lifted his hand to shield himself from the brightness that made his eyes water. He gasped at the fractured rainbows that covered the back of his hand before scattering across the snow. He turned in a half circle, amazed by the sparks of color in the frost at his feet.

Elly was outlined by the tree, which glittered with color—almost like crystalline wings at her back. The beauty of the tree—the beauty of *her*—took his breath away.

"It's a weeping willow," she said softly. She turned and parted the leaves with a tinkling sound. She slipped inside, her hand resting on the largest prism in the center of the trunk.

Adar was helpless to resist following her. "Have you heard the story about how the weeping willow came to be?" he said softly. She looked expectantly at him through the leaves. He circled the tree slowly, never taking his eyes off her. "Long ago, at the beginning of this age, there was a woman of the desert mountains. She was a skilled weaver, taking the goat wool and dying it into fantastic colors. Then she wove that wool into blankets and coats. Each one told a story.

"From far and wide, people came to buy her coats. The other weavers grew jealous—were their blankets not as bright and beautiful? Were their weaves not as tight? One night after drinking too much, they came to her cave, demanding to know why the people bought her blankets and not theirs. So she told them they weren't buying the blankets, they were buying the stories.

"This enraged them all the more, and they killed her. Not wanting her family to take vengeance upon them, they buried her body deep in the canyon.

"But weaving was in the woman's bones. Even in death, her spirit took hold of a seed and twisted and twined until a great tree grew up. One day, the woman's daughter saw the tree. It seemed to beckon to her with its branches, and it was a hot, miserable day. So the girl lay beneath the cool shade and fell fast asleep. And in her dreams, the branches wove the story of her mother's murder. The girl arose and told her family what had happened. Her family took their vengeance, hanging the murderers from the branches of the willow tree. And even today, if you lay beneath their bows, they will whisper secrets in your dreams."

Adar finished circling the tree and parted the branches to step inside. Elly watched him approach, her gaze unreadable. Every inch of her was covered in fractured rainbows, and her skin glistened with a thin layer of frost.

"Where—where did you hear such a story?" she asked a little breathlessly.

He chuckled as he came even closer. Close enough to reach out and tuck some of the curling hair behind her ears, though his hands stayed at his side. "My father collects stories like some people collect coins. He used to dole them out to us kids as payment for not giving him a headache by the end of the day. And I practically grew up in a library."

"You have a lot of siblings?"

"There are eighteen of us."

Elly's pretty mouth fell open. "Eighteen?"

"And that's if you don't count all my cousins and second cousins. And third. Never a shortage of sword partners for training."

"Swords? But I thought you were a navigator."

"Navigation I learned from the library and from my father. But where I'm from, every man is a warrior first." Adar's gaze fell on her mouth. She was smiling—the first real smile he'd ever seen from her. The rainbows from the prisms kissed her skin. He had the sudden urge to touch her face, to brush away the frost dusting her cheeks and see the girl beneath.

"You like it," she breathed.

Unable to resist any longer, he reached out and tucked her wild hair out of her face as an excuse to brush his fingers across her cheek. Her skin was soft, so soft, like he could sink into her. She closed her eyes at his touch, a soft sigh passing those lips. He leaned toward her.

"Elice!" called a sharp feminine voice.

Adar started, jerking away as if Elly's touch had burned him. She pushed him behind the tree while simultaneously stepping in front of him. He peeked around her but didn't see anyone.

"Quick," she said as she shoved him out from under the tree's boughs. He resisted—the tree was translucent, but at least it offered some cover. She silenced him with a look, her face screwed with concentration. As soon as he was out in the open, white stormed from her fingertips, forming a cone of snow around him.

He gaped at it openmouthed, the suspicion that had plagued him since he first met Elly snapping into place. Only the Winter Queen's daughter could have power over winter. But how could Elly be *the* princess? His reports said Princess Elice was forty years old, unattractive, and mean tempered. Elly—Elice—had been wearing rags when he'd first met her, and she lived in a cave. Or at least he'd thought she did.

He gritted his teeth. He'd been trying to get to the princess to accomplish his mission for days, and she was right in front of him the entire time.

The top of the cone hadn't even closed when the voice said, "Ah, there you are. I've been looking for you. I already checked that cave of yours."

Adar's head spun as he tried to remember if there was anything in that cave that pointed to his existence. He had to fight the urge to backpedal. Judging from the queen's voice, she was only a few steps from his current hiding place. He breathed shallowly, knowing any sound he made could alert her to his presence.

"Mother, I thought you'd be gone longer," Elice squeaked.

Her mother harrumphed. "I told you I'd be gone as long as it was necessary. What are you doing?"

"Just had an idea for a new tree."

Her mother didn't answer for a moment. "Is that the trunk?"

Adar heard the sharp zing of ice-fairy wings. The top of the cone finally sealed off just as a dozen fairy shadows passed over. Had they seen him? He waited, not daring to breathe, knowing certain fairies wouldn't need to see him. They would smell his presence. And if they figured out the unfamiliar smell was hiding inside the snow, he was as good as dead. Fire and burning, where were his swords when he needed them most!

"Yes," Elice said with a little more confidence. "I thought I'd go for an . . . amorphous shape."

Adar imagined Ilyenna looking the tree up and down. "Well, I came to tell you I'll be holding Chriel's hearing tomorrow morning. I want you to be there."

"Of course," Elice said quickly.

A brief pause. "Is this the tree you gifted me upon my return? Why didn't you tell me it cast rainbows?" Footsteps crunched through the snow, coming closer. "What made you think to make it?"

"The colors." Elice's voice was full of longing. "The only way to see bright colors here is with prisms."

A long sigh. "Are you so unhappy?" Elice didn't answer, and Adar imagined her hanging her head. "You know it wouldn't be safe for you anywhere my enemies could reach you," the queen went on. Adar frowned to himself as Elice kept her silence. "Walk back with me," her mother said. "I've prepared the Winter's End's feast for us, and I wanted to talk to you about your grandfather."

"You go ahead," Elice said. "I wanted to check on the seal before I head up."

Ilyenna made a disapproving sound. "I see the fox is gone."

Is that what Elice had told her mother she was healing—a fox? A predator, sure, but couldn't she have gone for something bigger? A polar bear, maybe.

"Yes," Elice answered. "He healed nicely."

Adar heard footsteps crunching in the snow and then the Winter Queen's voice. "Well, hurry along. Your grandfather and I will be waiting."

"I'll be right there."

Adar waited, wishing he could see what was going on just out of sight. Inside the frozen cocoon, he was safe from the wind, but the cold seeped through his clothing. He folded his arms around his chest, huddling to conserve body heat.

A moment later, the snow streamed away from him. He watched in amazement as it seemed to shrink into Elice and then disappear.

"It was you," he hissed. "The princess—all along, it was you?" This changed *everything*.

They stared at each other for a long time before he spoke again. "I thought I saw a spear of ice in your hand that day you killed the seal. Why did you lie to me?"

Elice looked away and shifted her weight from one foot to another. "My mother sank your ship . . . and I really didn't trust you."

"Probably smart of you." Adar climbed out, using the time to compose himself. Back in the sunshine, he brushed the loose snow off his shoulders and hair. "Where does it go—the snow?"

"Back to winter," Elice said. "The same from whence it comes."

He studied the forest this girl had made, realizing that for her, love and hurt went hand in hand. He clenched his teeth. It wasn't supposed to be like this. He wasn't supposed to care. "Is this how it always is for you? The never-ending cold?" Even he wasn't sure if he meant her mother or the weather.

Elice reached out and touched his cheek, and he could no longer feel the bite of winter. "It's not so bad for me. You have to produce heat to keep yourself warm. I don't."

That's how she'd kept him from freezing to death when he'd fallen in the ocean. Adar kicked himself—he'd seen signs of who she really was for days, but he'd written them off, all because he'd put too much confidence in the reports that placed the princess in her forties. And because, if he was honest with himself, he hadn't wanted Elly to be the princess.

He met her gaze. She stood straight and tall, her head back, determination in her eyes. This one was a warrior. Just like him. He steeled himself to remember that. Because this was war, whether Elice knew it or not. "Princess or not, you could still come with me. In the Summer Realm you'll see colors rich and bright and everywhere in between."

She reached out and pressed the pendant against her chest, then turned and started toward her cave. "Even if it was safe for me, I could never leave my grandfather." Adar felt sorry for her then, this girl who had everything and nothing at all. "But I will supply you with all that you need—food and warm blankets. You can even take a page from the atlas." She winced as she said the last. "All you have to do is find a Svass village. You'll be able to make your way home from there."

Huddled against the bitter breeze coming off the ocean, Adar again wished for the swords he'd lost in the shipwreck. He felt helpless without them. He was surprised when Elice tugged off his glove and took hold of his hand. The wind didn't feel bitter at all now. "I'm not sure I'll survive without you there to help me."

"Adar, if I disappear my mother will come looking."

"Perhaps you could convince her to let you go on a trip."

"She would never agree."

He took a deep breath, then let it out slowly. "You would be safer with me than here."

She gazed up at him, her expression unreadable. "Why?"

He reached out and took a prism, watching the fire spark inside. "Have you ever really crossed her—your mother?" Elice shook her head. "All the stories say how cruel and heartless she is," he said. Elice pulled her hand away and started down the rise, leaving him in the cold again. He pulled on his gloves and hurried after her.

"What stories do they tell?" she said evenly once he caught up.

Adar didn't want to speak ill of her mother—it was obvious Elice loved her—but he had a mission to accomplish. "That she killed her husband on their wedding night."

"That's ridiculous," Elice scoffed as she stepped into the shadows of her forest. "My father died when I was thirteen."

"Not your father—her first husband."

Elice stiffened. "First husband?"

Did she really not know? "He was a clansman—a Tyron, I think." Elice had stopped walking. Adar turned to watch her, a pattern of shadow and light from the distant sun frozen across her face.

She met his gaze with a glare. "It's a lie. It has to be."

"And the war she has raged for the last forty years?"

"Idara attacked first! My mother was only defending her people!"

Cold burst from Elice like daggers, burning him. He knew he should stop, but she needed to understand how dangerous the Winter Queen really was. How much pain she had heaped on the world. How at any moment she could turn on Elice and kill her too.

"She massacred hundreds of thousands of soldiers," Adar said firmly. "Not in defense, but in vengeance. If the Summer Queen hadn't stopped her, she would have annihilated all of Idara. And after all that, the Summer Queen has been the one to offer a truce and the Winter Queen has been the one to refuse it."

Elice pushed past him, storming toward the palace.

"Elly, she's unstable. It's only a matter of time before she hurts you too." He started after her.

Cold lashed out from her, practically shoving him back. "Go to the cave."

He halted just inside the darkness of the trees. He dared not get any closer to the palace. "His name was Darrien," he called after her. "Ask your mother. See if she denies it."

Elice paused, her shoulders rounded and her back to him. "It doesn't matter. My allegiance lies with the Winter Queen. She is a hard woman, but . . . she is my mother." Then Elice straightened and marched toward the castle without looking back.

8

As soon as Elice reached the palace, she collapsed beside one of a pair of trees that flanked the front steps. The trees were hard and leafless, with sharp branches that pierced the sky. The things Adar had said about her mother—how she was the reason the War of the Queens raged on. How she had murdered her first husband. That she was a danger to Elice. It had to be lies. All of it.

And yet . . .

Elice had witnessed the aloofness in her mother's gaze, tempered only by her father's love. And since he had died, Ilyenna had only grown more cold and distant. Elice knew well her mother's piercing anger—it had terrified her since she was a child. And the thought of it directed toward Chriel . . .

Elice shuddered. It wasn't what Adar had said that had shaken her to her core—it was the gleaming bits of truth shining through like stars on endless midwinter nights. And if it was true, could she really trust her mother? Could she risk staying behind when he left? And what of this Sundering? Her mother claimed it was caused by the Summer Queen, but Chriel and Adar both seemed to think that wasn't the case. And if they were right, Elice's mother's relentless pursuit of this war was causing it.

Elice curled up, her forehead resting on her drawn knees, and tried to rise above the fears swamping her. She wasn't sure how long she sat there, listening to the absolute silence of the Winter Queendom. Eventually, she unfolded herself and started up the stairs. Perhaps there was something to what Adar said. But he didn't know Elice's mother. Didn't see the other side to her. The side that brought Elice books. The side that fought against her dark nature.

Back inside the palace, Elice paused before entering the dining hall. She held up her hand and the ice shifted to snow, which she pulled into herself, creating a hole in the wall. She peered at the opposite wall, which was made up of enormous windows that were open to the fairies. A lengthy ice table stretched the width of the room. On it was the bounty of winter—meats of all kinds. There were fruits sweetened with winter's kiss—apples and rich-red and dark-purple berries. The light from thousands of candles shone off the reflective surfaces, giving a warm glow to the room.

The Winter Queen was pacing the length of the table, her hands intertwined behind her back. Her headdress of silver and diamonds and opals gleamed against her dark hair.

Elice's grandfather sat in his regular seat, watching his daughter. Deep circles lined his bloodshot eyes. "Ilyenna, we have to discuss this," he said. Snow swirled chaotically around her body. "I'm dying," he went on in a gravelly voice. "And Elice will be alone. You can't ignore that and hope it will go away." Elice felt the weight of the pendant, the chain heavy against the back of her neck.

Ilyenna paused in her pacing and sat in the chair beside him. "She has me. Is that not enough?"

"No," her grandfather said simply.

Elice's mother pinned him with a disbelieving stare. "Why?"

He reached out to lay a liver-spotted hand atop Ilyenna's pristine one. "Elice is lonely—terribly lonely. She needs companionship." Ilyenna opened her mouth to argue, but he shot her a look, and to Elice's disbelief, her mother held her peace. "All winter long, she'll be alone here. Months and months of darkness and silence."

Ever since Elice could remember, she'd been terrified of the dark.

Ilyenna sat perfectly still. "I always send her an aurora so she's not in complete darkness."

Otec studied his daughter. "Is that what you want for her? To live in near darkness for half her life—alone?"

Ilyenna's chin came up. "She would not be safe anywhere in summer. You know that."

Otec pulled his hand back and rested it atop his wooden cane. "Should she not know the touch of a man? The weight of her own children in her arms?"

"Having friends means having enemies," Ilyenna insisted. "And being in love means suffering heartache."

"Such is the way of the Balance. Life isn't perfect. Not even here."

Ilyenna spread her arms wide. "But here she is perfectly safe."

Her father sighed. "She would be safe with the highmen— the Svass are good people. Honest, hardworking. And in summer, when the Summer Realm has invaded their lands, she could bring her family here. Then you won't be alone either."

Ilyenna was silent a long time before she said, "Very well. I shall consider finding her a companion, someone trustworthy, and we will bring her here. That way my daughter will not be alone."

Elice's heart swelled. A friend. Perhaps Adar could stay after all. He would see that her mother wasn't as bad as the stories said. Then she could show him all of her world. If they were very, very careful, she could even take him swimming. He could meet her grandfather and Chriel.

"Ilyenna—" Otec began.

She shot him a warning look. "Is this not a compromise?"

He watched her for a moment. "For now."

Ilyenna took a dusty bottle of wine and poured three golden glasses. "Drink, Father. For we do not know how long my tardy daughter might be."

Elice iced over the small hole she'd created in the wall, counted to two hundred, folded her hands together to keep them from shaking, and stepped into the room. She studied her mother as memories danced through her head. Memories of flying in her mother's arms, her aurora wings around them. Walking hand in hand onto the ocean, ice freezing beneath their feet, so they could watch the orcas breech, their haunting calls like a lonely melody.

It was then that Elice had found her first patient. A bird with a broken wing, floating helplessly in the water. It was so exhausted it didn't even struggle as she picked it up. Tears had pricked her eyes. "Mother, can you help it?"

"For every rise, there must be a fall," her mother said serenely. "For every life, there must be a death. This is the way of the Balance."

Elice had turned tear-rimmed eyes to her. "Please. He's hurting—I can feel it."

"You could teach her," said Elice's father from behind them. "It would serve us well as we grow older."

Elice hadn't known what he meant, but her mother had said tightly, "I will teach her."

And she had, bringing Elice every book she could find on healing and herbs. She had brought the herbs, too, and encouraged Elice to practice—once even on a polar bear cub whose mother had died, though Ilyenna insisted a bear fairy stay with Elice to keep the animal from harming her.

Now her mother lifted her glass of winter wine, the movement distracting Elice from her memories. "Ah, there she is. Elice, thank you for the fresh meat. Come, sit beside me," her mother said, for once not mentioning Elice's tardiness. "We've had so little time to catch up since my return." Her grandfather sipped from his glass, watching them over the rim.

Ilyenna was not perfect, but she wasn't evil, either. With a relieved sigh, Elice sat beside her mother at the long table. Her grandfather leaned around his daughter. "For our gift today, your mother brought us apples from the clanlands—from the old tree behind the clan house."

Elice reached out and took a green apple. She marveled at the bright burst of color, a stark contrast to the silver, whites, grays, and blues of winter. The fruit crunched beneath her teeth, sourness and sweetness bursting across her tongue. They so rarely ever got to eat anything that didn't come from the ocean. She closed her eyes, wondering if there was anything in the world so lovely as apples.

She ate the entire thing, even the core, and then licked the juices from her fingers. "Are there any more?"

Her grandfather, who had been drinking his wine, choked a little and then laughed. "Yes, but we must save them. Your mother had to bargain with an apple fairy to get those out of season, just for us."

He stared at the bubbles forming in his delicate glass of wine, his gaze distant. "Your grandmother always traded for golden curry to put in her lamb stew. For dessert, she'd give us a bowl with raspberries, milk, and a dollop of honey. It was my favorite meal." Elice's grandfather, more than any of them, missed the world outside the queendom.

His gaze brightened and he chuckled. "When your mother was a girl, she used the berries to make her lips red. That was before she became a clanmistress."

"Father, there's no need to give my daughter ideas," Ilyenna chided, but there was a lightness to her voice. Qari landed on her mother's shoulder and whispered to the queen.

Adar's challenge flashed in Elice's mind. Determined to prove him wrong, she leaned around her mother and asked her grandfather, "What was she like, as a girl?"

"I've told you all the stories!" he proclaimed. Even one glass of wine made her grandfather very loud; Elice knew he was only pretending to be annoyed with her.

"Tell me again," she asked softly, desperate for any stories of the goodness to dispel the foulness of Adar's words. "Let it be my gift for today."

"But I had a lovely book to give you."

Elice wet her lips. "You could give me both?"

He shot a smile in his daughter's direction. "She was always trailing after her brother—learning to fight and hunt alongside him—when she should have been helping her aunt Enrid. But she was determined to be just as good as Bratton was." Bratton was Ilyenna's only sibling. The Summer Queen had killed him.

A mixture of fondness and sorrow showed on Otec's face.

Elice's mother waved off Qari and said to her father, "I was better than Bratton or Rone, and you know it."

Her mother's mention of Rone, Elice's father, rubbed at a deep ache in Elice's heart. It was painful, but in a good way.

"She was a healer, just as you are," her grandfather said with pride. "By the time she was fourteen, she was delivering babies all by herself. By the time she was sixteen, old aunt Enrid was too slow and blind to keep up the clanmistress duties. Your mother was still a child herself, but she took over. The other clanwomen listened to her—they trusted her."

Elice noticed a chip in one of the fine ice glasses. "Was there ever anyone else, Mother? Another boy, maybe? Or did you always love my father?"

Her mother sat back in her chair. "There was never anyone else."

Elice reached out and ran her finger along the glass's chipped rim, sucking in a breath when it sliced her finger. She watched the blood bead up, a splash of color against the paleness of her skin. "So there weren't any other men competing for your hand?"

Silence cut through the room. Her grandfather looked at her, his brow furrowed. "What do you mean?"

Elice watched as the bead of blood turned to ice and then dropped from her finger to land on her plate with a little clink. "Only, did Mother ever see any other boys?"

Her grandfather's gaze slid nervously to her mother and then he forced a laugh. "Who else could there be?" Something about the way her grandfather said it . . .

"Darrien." The name slipped past Elice's lips, and she immediately clamped them shut, hoping her mother hadn't heard. But the temperature in the room plunged, and jagged spears of frost spread rapidly out from her mother's chair.

"Where did you hear that name?" Ilyenna demanded coldly.

Grandfather's skin was mottled with anger, but there was fear in his gaze, too. "Elice, go to your room."

She started to rise, but her mother's voice froze her in place. "Where did you hear that name?"

Frost was forming on Elice's dress, climbing up her legs. It didn't hurt—winter never hurt her—but it frightened her. "I don't know," she breathed out. "I heard it somewhere, long ago, and I'm only now remembering." Suddenly she was aware of the utter silence in the room. She glanced around to find the winter fairies gone.

Lightning flickered in the distance, changing the light from soft to harsh in the space of a gasp. The fairies were already venting the Winter Queen's anger. Thunder rumbled. *By the Balance, Adar was telling the truth!* "Who is he?" Elice whispered. And then a terrible thought formed in her mind. "Was he my real father?"

Wind howled into the room, hurtling hard snow that stung Elice's exposed skin. Her mother's wings stretched out, growing along her back. She shot out one of the wide windows and into the rolling sky.

Her grandfather was breathing hard, his fists clenched. "You will never, ever say that name again, Elice. You will never even think it. Do you understand?"

She held up an arm to shield her eyes from the snow scouring her from all sides. Adar had been right about her mother's first husband. Did that mean the other things he'd said were true as well? Had her mother murdered Darrien and kept it a secret all these years? "I have a right—"

"You have no right!" her grandfather thundered. She hadn't seen him this angry since . . . well, ever.

"Was he my father?" Elice shouted, angry, but also wanting to be heard over the wind.

"No." Her grandfather stamped his cane down hard. "Fine. Ask your questions, because after this, we will never speak of it again."

"Was my mother married to a man named Darrien?"

Her grandfather winced. "It was a long time ago, Elly. But some wounds run so deep they never heal. We just learn to live with them."

"Did Mother really kill him?"

Her grandfather stared at her in shock. "How—"

By the Balance, she did! Elice realized. "Who was he?" One of the windows banged against the wall, the thin pane shattering into a thousand shards of ice.

When she looked back at her grandfather, she was shocked to see tears running down his weathered face, freezing almost as soon as they left his eyes and leaving his cheeks slick with ice. "He was a monster, Elice. A murderer and a rapist and a traitor." Her grandfather hunched over, resting his hands heavily on the table as if the words had exhausted him.

Elice's skin felt tender from the scouring wind that continued to howl outside. Already the room was covered in a blanket of ice, mounds revealing where plates and cups lay underneath. "So she killed him for it?"

"She wouldn't have had to if I had protected her." Elice's grandfather dropped his head as if it were too heavy to hold up. "Close the windows and clear up this mess."

Elice ran to do as he asked. As soon as a dozen windows were shut and the broken one repaired, she sucked all the snow into her, revealing frozen berries and apples, their vibrant colors muted by the cold. Her grandfather turned heavily and shuffled toward the door. She hurried to catch up with him and reached for his arm. "Grandfather—"

He pulled out of her grasp. "If you ever say that name to your mother or me again, I will never, ever forgive you." Her grandfather stepped out of sight beyond the door.

As if to accentuate his words, lightning flashed and thunder slammed so hard Elice jumped. All around her, the palace windows shattered. She hurried into the hall to see her grandfather cowering, broken ice all around him.

"Go to your room and lock the windows," he said. "It's going to be bad." She started after him, determined to make sure his windows hadn't broken, but he shrugged her off again. "Leave me be. I can take care of myself."

She watched him disappear out of sight before she broke into a run, rushing through the wailing storm that battered her from all sides. By the time she'd made it to her room, where she found the windows still intact, her sobs had started. She used all her strength to push her door shut against the wind. Tears fell from her eyes, turning to ice almost immediately. She pivoted and collapsed onto the soft blankets of her bed.

9

Elice wasn't sure how long she'd been lying there in the grainy darkness when she heard a voice. "Elly?"

She sat up in bed, her heart pounding. "Adar? What are you doing here?"

She could just make out the secret door opening and a shadowed form emerging. "I think the Queen of Winter is angry." His voice was shaking, his words stuttered.

Elice flung off the blankets and hurried toward him. "What's wrong?" But he didn't have to answer. The moment her searching fingers touched him, she noticed the bitter cold and immediately took it into herself.

He sagged against her side. "The blizzard suffocated the fire. And the temperature dropped so far and so fast . . ."

She should have realized he would be in danger in this kind of storm. She guided him toward her bed, encouraged him to lie down, and pulled her blankets over him. They weren't very warm, mostly just soft.

"I knew you wouldn't be able to resist me for long," Adar joked, his teeth chattering. "When we escape together, I have no doubt you'll fall completely under my spell."

Elice rolled her eyes and hurried to her closet, where she pulled out her white fur cloak. She rushed back to the bed and draped it across him. As she turned to find something else, his hand snaked out, grabbing hers. "Just don't let go of me. I'll warm up if you keep the cold back."

She hesitated, wondering how she would manage that. In the end, she moved a chair and sat near the bed, where she kept hold of his hand and watched as his shivering slowly subsided. Once he had relaxed, Adar said, "I assume you confronted your mother about Darrien."

Elice bit the inside of her cheek. "You were telling the truth, at least about some of it."

"Are you all right?" The teasing was gone from Adar's voice. When she didn't respond, he said, "Elly, I'm sorry."

She melted the frozen tears on her face and wiped them away with her free hand. "She's not evil. Her first husband was a bad man." Her mother's and grandfather's reactions to the very mention of Darrien's name had convinced Elice of that.

Adar shifted and sat up so his weight rested on one elbow. He seemed to study her face, and she thought he would push her more—try to convince her to abandon her family—but instead, he lay back down. "Have you heard the story of the Summer Queen's bargain?"

Elice shook her head. "I don't think I want to."

"Her whole family was starving," Adar began anyway. "She didn't think it could get any worse, and then her father went missing. When they finally found him, he was dying from a snakebite.

"She made a deal with the fairies to save his life. But the price had to be paid. A life had been spared, so the Balance decreed that another life must be taken. Nelay was taken to the temple to serve the Goddess of Fire. She never saw her family again."

Elice had never thought of Nelay as anything other than a raging dictator, and had certainly never imagined her as a starving child terrified for her father's life. Now Elice wondered if perhaps she had hated someone who didn't deserve it. "Why are you telling me this?" she asked.

"Because the Summer Queen isn't evil, either," Adar said.

Elice shook herself. It was just a silly story, probably exaggerated. And perhaps not even true. "How do you know so much?" she asked warily?

"They teach Nelay's history in their temples."

Elice glanced up at Adar, wishing she could make out his expression in the darkness. "You've been to Idara?"

"Many times."

"Why would you go there?"

He shifted a little. "My uncle is a smuggler. He used to take me with him sometimes."

"What's it like?"

"Arid and windy, but during the game of fire, the city is bright with braziers and torches. Everyone goes to see the game played out at the temple grounds. There's dancing and singing and games and parades, and more food than you could ever eat."

By then, Elice was sitting back, his hand nestled in her lap. The silence after the rich cadence of his voice rang with possibility instead of emptiness. "Tell me more."

He did—one story after another as the storm raged on beyond her icy windows. She let go of his hand just long enough to get them water, made of the melted snow she collected outside her window.

When Adar's voice was scratchy from talking so much, Elice told him her own stories. Stories she'd learned from the hundreds of books she had read. Stories she'd heard from her grandfather. Adar's hand was warm and rough in her grasp, and that warmth spread throughout her, leaving her drowsy.

"Is this blizzard going to let up anytime soon?" he asked with a yawn.

Elice glanced outside, at the storm that still blasted her windows—a manifestation of her mother's rage. "Not for a long while."

"Are you going to sit in that chair all night?"

She shifted to look at the dark shadow that made up Adar's face against the backdrop of her white bedding. "What else do you suggest?"

"It has to be nighttime now."

She didn't argue with him. She knew her body rhythms. It was well after the time she usually went to bed.

"Sleep beside me," he said.

Elice huffed. "I may have grown up isolated and alone, but I am not ignorant to the lusts of men."

"Lusts?" There was laughter in Adar's voice. "Elly, I just want to sleep without freezing to death. And I don't want you spending the whole night in that uncomfortable chair when you could just as easily be sleeping too."

She shot him a dubious look that he probably couldn't see. "I'm not sure I believe you."

"If you don't help me, Elly, I'm going to freeze to death. Even if I had dubious intentions, would I risk dying for them? You could kill me with a thought."

She rested one of her arms on her stomach. "I know how men are. My mother has told me all about them."

Adar looked up at the ceiling. "Was your father a cruel man?"

Gaze averted, Elice shook her head.

"What about your grandfather?"

"Of course not!" she burst out. "But I know them. And my mother was right." Elice thought of the husband who had hurt her. "There are evil men in the world."

Adar tugged down his silly hat. "But there are more good and honorable men. And your mother's doing you a disservice if she only tells you about the bad people."

As Elice considered his words, her resolve wavered. She had a choice. She could believe him or her mother. She thought of Adar. Of his scars, the reverent way he touched her books, the mischief in his eyes, not to mention his slicked-back hair and somewhat large forehead. She thought of the way he'd looked at her when she'd shown him her willow tree, with an awe that had quickly faded to something soft, even gentle. Despite all his flaws, he was sort of pleasant to look at. And she thought he might even be her friend.

What if her mother had told her the world was dangerous and cruel just to keep her trapped here? What if the world wasn't a place of darkness and debauchery, but color and light? Elice took a deep breath and let it out slowly, determined to relax. "First, apologize."

"For what?" Adar asked carefully.

"For what you said about my mother."

He hesitated. "My mother says men should apologize frequently, even without cause. So I'm sorry."

"You need to work on that."

"I'm sorry," he said, immediately this time.

Elice couldn't help but laugh. She considered going to bed fully dressed, but she doubted she'd ever get comfortable enough to sleep. So she unbuckled her clan belt and tugged off her overdress, then laid both across the back of the chair. She added the pendant her grandfather had given her to the top of the pile.

She went to the other side of the bed and eased under the covers. Adar hissed through his teeth. "Don't let all the cold in."

"Sorry," she mumbled as his searching hand found hers. On her back—as far away as she could get while still holding his hand—she stared straight into the darkness, her whole body ridged. His big fingers pinched her smaller ones. Elice adjusted her hand position so their fingers weren't woven together, but resting one on top of the other. That was much better. But she still couldn't seem to relax.

"You try anything, and I'll freeze your balls," she said suddenly.

Adar choked on a laugh. "I promise."

Exhausted as she was, it took her a long time to fall asleep.

Elice lay in a field, the warm sun beating down on her cool skin, an insect crawling around the inside of her wrist. All around her a sea of grass shifted and rustled with the gentle breeze. Birdsong trilled from somewhere out of sight. She breathed deep the smell of soil and growing things. Even though she knew she was dreaming, she wanted to stay forever. To never awake.

She wasn't sure how long she lay there, but eventually the prickly grass was replaced with granular snow. The warmth of the sun became the chilled kiss of winter. The grass and the sound of the birds were replaced with silence.

Elice woke thinking the dream was more a memory than something conjured by her imagination. But where would she have ever experienced summer? Then she realized something warm and heavy rested on her hand. Remembering the night before, her eyes shot open. She and Adar both lay on their sides, facing each other. His chiseled face was only inches from hers. He still wore the ridiculous hat, had even managed to snugly tie the strings under his chin. Her eyes swept over the dark stubble on the lower half of his cheeks—darker in the cleft in his chin. His dark lashes and full lips. And a nose that was a little on the big side.

She glanced past him at the snow that had sifted through the tiny cracks around the windows and piled in soft mounds along the walls and out onto her floor. After double checking to make sure he was really asleep, Elice slipped from the bed, opened a window, and concentrated on clearing away the snow from her room and her balcony. As she worked, she thought of Chriel. It was the fairy's last day of captivity. After this, she would be free. Elice's excitement and relief was tempered by the fact that hiding Adar was about to get that much harder.

Outside, she studied the landscape, transformed from yesterday's storm. Her ice forest was completely covered, only a few mounds hinting at the massive trees beneath. Later, she'd have to remove the snow as well as repair any damaged trees. Beyond the forest, the shoreline was frozen waves of shuga ice, the kind formed in choppy waters. Farther out, the ocean was a soup of slush and frazil ice, a slush of needle-like ice crystals that had an almost oily sheen.

At the sound of rustling behind her, Elice turned to see Adar shiver and pull the cloak higher over his shoulders. She stepped back into the room and shut the door, cutting off the breeze, and he settled immediately, breathing deeply.

Suddenly she knew what she was going to make for him. She formed it quickly. Then, not satisfied with the result, she set it aside and started again. When she had it exactly how she wanted it, she opened herself fully to winter and splintered off a trickle of the magic, bonding it to the ice. That way it would never melt.

She moved close and studied the stubble on Adar's cheeks, her hand hovering above his skin. She wanted to know what it felt like—that stubble. If it would be soft like the hairs on her legs, or coarse like wool. Feeling brave, Elice touched his cheek, automatically drawing the cold away. The hair was coarse and rough, almost like crystallized snow.

She realized something. She'd been regularly touching Adar for only a day, yet she had come to crave the contact. The warmth of his skin. She tried in vain to remember the last time her mother had touched her more than briefly.

Adar's eyes flew open, and she jerked her hand back. He watched her, his brows drawn. "For Winter's End," she said in a rush. "We give each other gifts every day. And when you asked me to make you something, it reminded me that you haven't had any gifts. So I made something for you." She realized she was rambling and clamped her mouth shut. She held out a wicked-sharp dagger, complete with a sheath of decorative snow. "Neither will ever melt."

He made no move to take her gift, and the moment stretched out awkwardly. Elice's hand had just started to fall in dejection when he finally reached out and took the dagger from her. He unsheathed the blade and stared at the razor edge. Ever so carefully, he attached it to the clan belt that had been her father's.

Elice folded her hands in her lap, and in her embarrassment, winter opened up inside her. She reached for the comforting touch, and almost without realizing what she was doing, she drew a sliver toward her. The ice was malleable in her hands, like clay. She pressed down with her thumbs, flattening it. Her fingers pinched off the ends and formed three curving petals and three with sepals. Then she curled the petals inward to create a flower bud that fit nicely on her palm and looked almost like a flame.

She held it out to him. "I was named after the elice blossom." Adar stared at the flower, his mouth a thin line. "I know it's rather simple, but I always wanted you to have a fire with you, even if it won't actually keep you warm."

She stared at the floor, trying to force down the hurt that he didn't seem to want her gifts. She went to her clothes from the day before and started dressing.

"Thank you, Elly, for these gifts," she heard him say. "I cannot tell you how perfect they are. But I don't have anything to give you in return."

So that's why he hadn't wanted her gifts. She let out a silent sigh of relief. "My grandfather often gives me stories as gifts."

"I've already given you plenty of those," Adar said.

Now fully dressed, she approached the bed. His gaze went to the pendant at her throat. "I haven't seen that before. It's interesting."

"My grandfather made it a long time ago for my grandmother."

Adar folded one hand behind his head and stared at the ceiling. "You know, someday our children will talk about the ice knife their mother gave their father to show how madly in love with him she really was."

Elice threw her boot at him and missed. But she wasn't really angry or even all that embarrassed. She was growing used to his teasing.

He sighed. "I want to give you more than just stories, Elice. I would give you your freedom, if only you would come with me."

She held out her arms. "Am I not free now?"

"Not to become what you were born to be. You're too busy satisfying everyone else's needs."

She turned away from him, staring out at the clouds on the horizon. They were nacreous clouds, like streams of molten copper, silver, and rose-gold. "Come with me."

Adar pushed himself out of the bed. "Where are we going?"

"Outside. My mother and her fairies will be exhausted after the storm last night. Which means they won't be out and about for hours yet."

They went down the stairs and hurried to the cave. Elice pulled the mounds of fine snow into herself and sent it to winter.

"Does it drop on someone's head when you do that, or simply disappear entirely?" Adar asked.

She frowned. "I don't really know where the snow goes."

He looked around the cave. "And how did you get lucky enough to find this place, with an opening that points straight toward the winter palace?"

She reached out and picked up a piece of volcanic rock. She filled it with ice, then thawed it over and over. On about the fifth time, it crumbled in her hands.

"Huh," was all Adar said.

Brushing off her hands, Elice approached Picca, who was chirping for attention. Elice entered the pen and eased back the bandages. She almost felt sad to see the dark scars. "You should be free." She choked a little and had to press the back of her hand to her mouth. Picca's purpose in life couldn't be to wait for Elice to bring her food and touch her. The seal deserved to push through the waves, hunt her own food, and someday have pups of her own. "I can't wait to watch you swim."

Adar stepped up to the pen. "Why save something you might only hunt later? Something that will only hurt you when you have to let it go?"

"Because she needed me. For the time I've had her, she has brought me joy. And now I can set her free."

Elice disintegrated the rest of the cage. Then she went to the table, took the scraps of meat, and lured the seal after her. Picca was far too big for her to carry. "This way I can balance out some of the lives I have to take in order for us to survive."

They stepped into the brilliant sunshine. Adar gaped at drifts taller than he was. Elice simply sucked in the snow to reveal the trees hidden beneath it. She studied them, occasionally reaching out to fix a broken branch or add a leaf that had blown off.

"Fire and burning," he muttered. "When your mother loses her temper, she really loses her temper."

"You should have seen her after Father died," Elice said quietly. "The whole palace was buried under drifts of snow, and the roof was groaning under the weight. I'm not sure we would have survived at all if Chriel hadn't gotten through to my mother that she was about to crush her own father and daughter."

"Maybe I should meet this Chriel and she could convince the queen to let me go," Adar said evenly.

A pang of worry shot through Elice for her friend. "That isn't likely. She's fallen out of favor with my mother and has been locked up in the cellar. My mother promised she'd let Chriel go though, as long as she apologizes at the hearing."

"Apologize for what?" Adar almost sounded nervous.

Elice turned to him. "At the celebration, she told stories about the Sundering. Mother thinks it's all just stories to undermine her. She's worried her fairies will turn on her like the summer fairies turned on their queen."

"Those aren't just stories, Elice. I've seen it. I've known people who have died from it."

"You don't know the Summer Queen like I do," Elice pointed out. He snorted and she shot him a glare. "She's a master manipulator, Adar. This is exactly the kind of thing Nelay would do. And my mother wouldn't lie to me."

He was speechless. Elice looked up at him, not bothering to hide the tears in her eyes, and said, "You don't understand. If what you say is true, it's my fault."

"What is?"

"The Sundering."

His brows rose. "That's ridiculous." He reached out to her, but she moved away, leaving him staring after her. "Elly," he called after her.

"What do you want from me, Adar?" she replied, not even turning her head.

He hurried to catch up with her. "Elice, I—" Trying very hard not to cry, she watched him shove his hands in his armpits, his shoulders hunched against the cold. Then he bumped her with his good shoulder and teased, "I heard they had to take all the furnishings from the Summer Queen's room because she kept lighting things on fire when she was angry."

Elice forced a laugh, relieved he'd let it drop. Glad he was trying to make her smile. "Where do you hear all these stories?"

He grinned. "I told you, my father is a historian. He's fascinated by stories of the fairies and their queens."

Elice glanced at the sky and realized she only had a few more hours until Chriel's hearing. Then her friend would be released. Elice would never be able to hide Adar from Chriel—the rabbit fairy was far too perceptive. And far too loyal to her queen.

Elice shifted her gaze to Adar. "You'll need to go soon. Once Chriel is released, I won't be able to hide you for long. Not from her."

"Going to miss me, are you?" His tone was light, but his eyes were sad.

Picca was lagging, so Elice tossed her a bit more meat to keep her interested. The seal chewed happily, not seeming bothered at all by the snow coating the meat. "I don't want you to go," Elice murmured.

She half expected Adar to ask her to come with him again, but he didn't. He only grasped her hand and said, "You know I can't stay here."

All the breath left Elice in a rush. "Actually, I think you could. I overheard my grandfather and my mother last night— I'm to have a companion. Why couldn't that companion be you?"

Before he could respond, they passed through the last of the trees and rounded the rise. Elice bent down and wrapped her arms around Picca. She couldn't stop the tears now. "I'm going to miss you."

Picca bumped Elice's cheek with her nose. Sniffing, Elice stood and cleared a path all the way down the water, and then started working on the beach. Picca saw the ocean in the distance and didn't need any more persuading. She hunched along, her fat jiggling. But she paused at the edge of the water to look back.

"Go on," Elice whispered. Picca slipped into the slushy water, free in a way Elice never would be.

Adar studied her face and then wrapped his arm around her. She rested her head on his shoulder. "You would want for nothing—rooms, clothing, jewels. My mother would make you impervious to the cold. You would be safe from the battles that gave you all those scars. We could swim in the ocean and watch the whales. And in the winter, you could see the auroras and we could read books by candlelight. I know you'd be leaving—"

"Elice . . ."

She could hear the "no" in the way he said her name, and she couldn't bear for him to reject her so quickly. "Don't answer now. Just think about it."

"Elice, thinking about it won't change my answer."

She wiped the tears from her cheeks. "Oh." She moved out from under his arm.

He sighed. "Even if your mother would let me stay, I couldn't have a life without purpose, without meaning."

Elice clenched her jaw. "Is that what you think of me?"

He tugged on his ridiculous hat. "You make all these incredible things—the palace, the ice forest—but no one ever sees them. No one ever appreciates them. You don't touch anyone else's lives. You don't influence anyone for the better." Shaking his head, he looked away. "I couldn't live a life where I didn't make a difference—where no one even knew I existed."

His words hurt more than if he'd slapped her. Her eyes fluttered closed, sending twin tears plunging down her cheeks. "So my life isn't important?"

"Doesn't matter what I think," Adar said softly. "What do you think? What do you want out of your life? Because if this is it" —he gestured to the palace— "then stay."

Elice ached for the life he spoke of—a life where she mattered. But what of her grandfather and mother? "I love my family too much to leave them."

"Yes, and what about them? Do they love you enough to let you go? Like you let Picca go?"

"If I left the queendom, I would never be safe." Elice stared at the dark ocean and wondered what it felt like to be cold. If it was bitter, dark, and empty. If so, then she'd never known anything else. "I know you want me to come with you, but I can't."

"Maybe you're right. Maybe it's better if you stay."

"What?" She was surprised at her dismay over Adar's words.

His gaze was locked on the horizon, his expression conflicted. "You wouldn't be safe. And . . . I couldn't bear for you to be hurt."

It pained her that he'd been so easy to convince. Which was ridiculous. "I have to go," she told him. "Mother is pardoning Chriel this morning, and I have to be there."

They turned without a word and slipped through a tunnel of mounded snow, only the muted sky and the palace in the distance visible. "You can't come to my rooms anymore, Adar. Chriel would see you for sure."

After a pause, he said, "I'm running low on wood."

They stepped into the cave, where Elice's vision turned the shadows blue after the brilliance of before. "I'll try to get you more," she replied.

Inside the cavern, she started toward the secret door, but Adar took hold of her hand and reached out with his other palm to cup her face. She closed her eyes. He was going to leave. Soon. The realization hit her with such force she felt dizzy.

"Elly, there's something I need to tell you," he whispered.

She shook her head and hurried toward the door. "I can't go and you can't stay. There isn't anything more to say."

10

S ituated in a high-back chair between her mother and grandfather, Elice watched the thousands of fairies, a smattering
of animal and magic bonded to form creatures that could
have been human, had there been any humanity left to them.
Elice realized how desperately she needed Chriel's steadying
presence, her gentle demeanor.

Two raptor fairies came into the room in their bird forms,
carrying an iron cage between them. Inside, Chriel stood with an
ageless stillness. Elice's heart lurched. She'd missed her friend.
Missed learning the secrets of the world in their library while the
candles flickered and the aurora danced beyond the open windows.

The raptors set the cage on the long table before them without so much as a lurch before shifting into fairies with sharp
beaks and talons. They backed away without a sound.

The Winter Queen studied the rabbit fairy. "Perhaps I
should kill you, Chriel." She looked about the room, a warning
in her gaze. "It would certainly strike fear into the hearts of my
enemies."

Elice stiffened. Was her mother about to change her mind?

Ilyenna let out a long breath. "But really, how could they possibly fear me more than they already do? Those who rise against me believe I am unbendable and unforgiving, and it is true that the magic in my veins does not lend itself to mercy."

Her voice dropped. "But my father and daughter have tempered my need for justice. Chriel, you have faithfully served me and my family these long years. And even a Winter Queen can be capable of mercy. Beg my forgiveness, declare your allegiance, and I will spare you."

Ilyenna pulled out a key, inserted it in the cage door, and swung it open. Chriel stepped out, her feet bare and dirty. Her face was haggard, her body limp. Being underground had left her exhausted and weak. Elice longed to comfort her friend, but she dared not show any sympathy for the fairy her mother was trying to make an example of.

"I thank you for your mercy, my queen," Chriel said.

Elice breathed a sigh of relief. When this was over, things could go back to the way they were. Adar's chaotic presence would be gone, and Elice would resume her studies and her life. So why did she feel so lost?

Chriel took a deep breath. "I thank you, but I cannot partake of it."

Many things happened at once: Elice gasped, dozens of the fairies in the room shifted to their animal forms, and Grandfather shot a worried look at Elice.

Ilyenna rose to her feet, leaned forward, and placed her hand on the table, ice spreading from her fingertips. "What did you say?"

Chriel lifted her head. "This age will end in blood and fire. That end comes, close enough I can taste the ash in my mouth. Your reign is nearly over, my queen. Our allegiance must shift to another if we are to survive."

The table beneath Ilyenna's hands cracked in half, the two pieces wedging against one another at a harsh angle. Elice jumped back. Chriel fluttered her wings, which were a little out of sync, so she wobbled in the air. Ilyenna lifted her hand, a ball of icy light appearing above her palm.

"No!" Elice cried, lunging at her mother. But the Winter Queen threw out her opposite hand and formed a wall of ice between them, bisecting the dais. Elice clawed at the slick ice.

"Chriel," Ilyenna said, her voice dead, "for your treachery, I revoke your ability to transfer, and I grant you the one true death."

"No!" Elice screamed, banging on the ice and trying to disintegrate it. But her mother kept her hand outstretched, reforming the ice faster than Elice could destroy it.

Ilyenna threw the ball of silvery light at Chriel. For one brief moment, the rabbit fairy was like liquid silver, beautiful and glorious. She stiffened, her regal wings flapping at her back while her gaze shifted to Elice. "Outshine the darkness," Chriel told her.

And then the fairy shattered into a thousand shards of ice.

Something pierced Elice's cheek, hard and sharp and impossibly cold. No one spoke. No one moved. Even the fairies seemed terrified. Elice stared at the shattered ice that used to be Chriel. "You—you murdered her," Elice said in disbelief.

Lowl flew forward, her gray tail twitching. "A traitor, no doubt recruited by the treacherous Queen of Summer. We must end this."

Ilyenna nodded slowly. "It has to be the Summer Queen's doing."

Behind the thick wall of wavering ice, Elice glared her mother. "I hate you." She hadn't meant to say the words. They were just there.

Her mother turned to regard her with a cool expression. "I'll get you a better gift than Chriel's life. A few dozen books. Boxes of herbs."

"I don't want more books!" Elice screamed.

Her mother waved a dismissive hand. "Take her out, Father."

Elice's grandfather took hold of her shoulder—she hadn't even realized he'd come to stand behind her—but Elice shrugged him off and lowered her head. She opened herself completely to winter. It raged inside her as it had never raged before. The castle walls trembled, bits of ice breaking off and falling down with a sound like breaking glass. She sucked in the barrier of ice that separated her from her mother. Faster and faster.

Her mother turned to her with wide eyes. "And what are you going to do when you reach me, Elice?"

Her grandfather laid a gentle hand on her shoulder. "Elly."

Elice lowered her hand and whirled around. Feeling the need to destroy something, she blasted the icy doors and walked through the shards with her head high. She heard her grandfather hobbling after her as fast as he could. At the tinkling of ice, she whirled to see the door reforming under her mother's magic. Elice glared at the queen as she slowly disappeared behind the thick ice. With a thud, a huge bar dropped across the doors.

Elice raised her fingers to her cheek and removed the sliver that had once been a part of Chriel. She felt blood bubble up and trickle down her face before it froze on her chin.

Her grandfather stood very still, both hands braced on his cane. "I'm sorry, Elly."

Elice backed away from him. Winter raged inside her, so close to the surface that she was afraid she would really hurt her grandfather if he touched her. "Do you still believe in her goodness?" she asked him.

His shoulders drooped. "Sometimes winter takes over, and she's not your mother anymore. She would have hurt you had you tried to interfere."

Elice gave a bitter laugh. "She's not my mother at all." She pivoted on her heel and marched away.

"Don't say that," her grandfather called after her.

"Chriel was right! Ilyenna should no longer be queen!"

"The only way to unseat a queen is to kill her. You know that."

Elice whipped around. "The War of the Queens has been raging for longer than I can remember. If my mother was dead, it would stop."

Her grandfather's eyes glittered with anger. "And what do you think would happen to you if she dies? With the powers of winter, you are a threat to any future queen. One she would end easily."

Elice backed away from him. "Would I be in any more danger from a stranger than my own mother?"

"Are you willing to take the chance?"

"Chriel was right, Grandfather, and we both know it."

"You better hope she wasn't."

Elice walked away with a measured cadence. When she opened the door to her room, she was surprised to see Adar there. He jumped off her bed, atlas in hand.

"I know you told me not to come in here anymore, but the wood is completely out and I think there is a way we could hike out of—" He stopped, his expression changing to one of concern. "Elice, why are you bleeding?"

She rushed to her wardrobe and jerked open the doors, then grabbed her satchel and stuffed in a change of clothes. Next she went to her bed and stripped off the blankets. "We're leaving. Now."

"Chriel?"

Elice staggered as the pain of losing her friend slammed into her again, but this time without anger or disbelief to curtail it. She hunched over, gasping. "My mother killed her."

"Fire and burning, no." Adar came toward her. Elice held out her hand to stop him. "Don't—don't touch me." With the cold raging from her, she didn't trust herself not to hurt him.

Dropping his hands to his sides, he nodded. Elice wiped her nose on her sleeve and said, "We'll head west, along the coast until it curves to the south. There are villages farther southwest. If we can get on a boat we'll be all right."

Adar watched her with concern, his hands hovering as if he thought she might pass out. "Your mother will send the fairies after us."

"I can protect us from the fairies," Elice scoffed.

"And from your mother?"

Elice slung her satchel over her shoulder. "She can't force me to come back." Realizing he was probably more worried about himself than her, she said, "I won't let her hurt you. I swear I won't."

He advanced on her with the same carefulness she used when approaching a wounded animal. "Are you sure you want to do this? Because there might not be any coming back."

She looked up into his dark eyes. "I never want to come back." Very slowly, he reached out. "Don't—"

"You won't hurt me, Elly." He took hold of her arms and pulled her to him. She collapsed against his chest, and even through all the layers of his clothes, the warmth of him was overwhelming. Soft and yielding, yet strong and right at the same time. She fit here—her body molding itself to his.

Adar pulled back and looked into her eyes. "What if you knew you were going to be captured by the Summer Queen? Would you still go?"

Elice steeled herself. "I would be no more of a prisoner with the Summer Queen than with my own mother." He looked at her a long time, indecision on his face. She clenched her hands into fists. "I'm going. You don't have to come, though you won't survive without me."

He reached out and tucked a stray strand of her wild hair behind her ear. "I know a warrior's heart when I see one. I'll stick with you." Elice didn't understand why he seemed so sad when he said it.

The pain of Chriel was still there in her heart, still overwhelming, but there had to be a way through it. A way beyond it. And Elice had a purpose now.

Just then, a startled gasp sounded from the door. Before Elice could even think, Adar had shoved her behind him—a stupid move, since he was the one who needed protecting.

"Elice," came the voice of her grandfather.

She emerged from behind Adar, her hands up to encourage them both to stay calm. "Grandfather, this is Adar—he's one of the men from the ship Mother sank. I found him. I've been caring for him."

"The fox," her grandfather said.

Elice nodded. "I'm going with him. And—and I'm not coming back."

Her grandfather quickly shut the door behind him. "I'm sorry about Chriel, but this . . ."

It was still too raw for Elice to talk about. "I won't be a prisoner here anymore, Grandfather. I have to go."

He watched her with his filmy gaze. "I know." She blinked at him in surprise. She'd expected arguments. "I've been trying to get your mother to let you go for a few years now."

"You have?"

Otec sighed and stiffly lowered himself onto one of her chairs, then rested his hands atop his cane. "Your soul shines too bright not to share, Elice." His gaze swung to Adar. "But I'm not convinced this is the way to leave. Do you even know this man?"

Adar inclined his head. "I am her friend."

Her grandfather made a sound low in his throat. "What was your ship doing in the Winter Queendom in the first place?"

"We were lost in a storm and couldn't navigate because of cloud cover."

"So you were lost? Very convenient."

Elice sighed. "Grandfather, he knows who I am. He knows I could freeze him with a thought. I can take care of myself."

Her grandfather's gaze softened as he looked at her. "Sometimes men only show you what they want you to see, Elice. Believe me, there are other ways he can hurt you."

She swallowed an angry retort. "Mother will never let me go. You know that. This is the only chance I will ever have."

Otec pursed his lips and studied her for a long time. "You will do this with or without my help?"

"Yes, I will."

"Very well." He rose to his feet, kissed her forehead, and started toward the door.

"Grandfather, what do you mean to do?"

He turned back to her. "I'm going to try to save this young man's life." Elice shot Adar a nervous look. Her grandfather sighed. "I can't make any promises, but she is my daughter. Sometimes she forgets that. It's time to remind her." He studied Adar. "I hope you are as honorable as my granddaughter seems to think you are."

"I will do whatever I can to help her."

"Even if that means letting her go?" Elice's grandfather said quietly.

Adar's brow furrowed and he slowly nodded. "Even then."

Unable to stand it anymore, Elice darted forward and embraced her grandfather. The pendant he'd given her was a painful lump between them. He squeezed her and whispered, "I love you, my Elly girl."

"I love you too," she said. And then he was gone, leaving another aching hole in Elice's chest. For all that she was going toward, it seemed she was leaving more behind.

"Let's go," she said to Adar. "Before my mother discovers we're gone."

11

Hand in hand, they raced down the front stairs of the palace. The movement jostled Adar's shoulder, but he only gritted his teeth and kept moving. He didn't try to cover his face. A confrontation was looming no matter what they did. Now more than ever, he wished for the comforting weight of his swords—even if those swords would be next to useless against the Queen of Winter.

Just as they left the sheltered grove of Elice's ice trees, an aurora shot through the sky above them. The snow reflected bizarre green shimmers. Elice whirled around, pushing Adar behind her. He let her. Here, she was the one with the power. Though it rankled him, he kept his good arm at his side.

In the sky, green lights shifted like a current curving around a rock. In the center of that current, he saw her, the Winter Queen. She wore white, and her hair had the same wavy tangles as her daughter's. They shared the same large eyes and full lips. But where Elice was emotive and eager to please, Ilyenna's expressions were all harsh lines and sharp edges.

The woman landed in a crouch before them. Her gaze locked with Adar's. In her eyes he saw a raging blizzard that seemed to scourge him from the inside out. He held tighter to Elice, silently asking her to take the cold beating down on him.

"Elice," Ilyenna said, her voice warbling as if she was barely in control. "What have you done?"

"I'm leaving, Mother. And I won't be coming back."

Her mother rose regally to her feet with the smooth grace of a barely leashed predator. "Chriel was a traitor—"

"She was more of a mother to me than you have ever been!" Elice cried, her touch suddenly sending freezing barbs through Adar's hand. He jerked free and cradled it against his chest, his fingers already numb and heavy. He should have realized how close she was to losing control.

"You have no idea how hard I have to fight to retain any scrap of humanity." Ilyenna's nostrils flared and cold radiated off her in waves, piercing Adar's thick clothing as if he wore rags.

He studied Elice, whose beauty was exemplified in everything she touched, and he wondered how that touch had failed to penetrate her mother's fierceness. How lonely Elice must have been, lost here in the dark. Suddenly, his anger toward her mother roared inside him like a bonfire. "Well, you failed," he shouted. "You're more fairy now than—"

Ilyenna made a flinging motion with her hand, slamming a raging blizzard into him. Adar staggered back several steps before he could brace himself. Pain lanced through his shoulder. Hand up to protect his face from the snow flaying him alive, he struggled forward a couple steps, blinded by the storm.

"Elice!" he cried.

Then the wind stopped. Elice was trapped in a cage of icicles. With one flick of her wings, the queen stood before Adar. He staggered back, holding in his grimace of pain as she studied him, calm as death. "So you are why my daughter has turned against me."

"Don't hurt him!" Elice screamed.

Adar felt real fear then, for Ilyenna was endless and inhuman. But he was a warrior—one of the finest in his realm. He squared his shoulders. "Let her go."

Ilyenna's gaze narrowed. "You cannot trust this man, Elice. You can't trust any of them."

The ice binding Elice flickered to snow that immediately turned back to ice. "I trust him more than I trust you!" she screamed.

Ilyenna shook her head. "I have warned you—all my life I have warned you."

"And because of that, I have been safe." Elice's words dripped with bitterness. "But the price of that safety is that I have never known warmth. Never felt the grass beneath my feet. Never smelled a real tree. I've never had a friend I shared secrets or gossip with. Never laughed myself silly. I would trade one day of that for a thousand years here."

In that moment, Adar swore he would find a way to give Elice at least some of those things before his mission was through. Then Ilyenna's chin came up and she reached toward him. He tensed, waiting for the cold to suck his life away, but her fingers gently brushed across his cheek. Adar thought of the dagger Elice had given him. But though he was fast, he knew the queen's cold was faster.

"I could kill him," Ilyenna murmured. "And then you would forget such ridiculous fantasies. You would come home and things will be as they were."

"Things will never be as they were." Elice had finally stopped struggling. "And if you hurt him, I will never forgive you."

Ilyenna finally looked at her daughter. "Very well. I will agree to let him go. We will never speak of this day again. And you will stop this little . . . rebellion of yours. You see how merciful I am?"

Then Elice would never be free. It was foolish, so very foolish, but Adar drew his dagger and lunged at the queen. Ilyenna didn't even look at him as a blast of wind hit him and threw him back. His back crashed into one of Elice's trees so hard it shook, sending delicate prisms cascading down around him. The pain in his shoulder was momentarily blinding. Dizzy and reeling, he tried to get to his feet, but his body refused to cooperate.

"I told you, Elice, you cannot trust them." Ilyenna stalked toward Adar, her hands shifting to a brilliant silver-white.

"No!" Elice screamed at the same time another voice said, "Ilyenna, let him go!"

Elice's grandfather was gasping for breath as he emerged from the edge of the forest. He came up short as icicles fell from the sky, impaling the ground around him and trapping him. "Ilyenna, stop!"

The Winter Queen walked calmly to Adar and cocked her head as she looked down at him. "What game are you playing with my daughter?"

"I swear," Elice sobbed, "if you kill him I'll throw myself from the towers!"

Pretty sure he wouldn't survive this encounter, Adar tried to catch his breath. Might as well tell the queen what he thought of her and how she treated her daughter. "I've been her friend. Which is more than I can say of you."

The Winter Queen's gleaming hands twitched. "Elice has no inkling of the guile of men. I will not allow any harm to come to her." She bent down, stretching toward him. Adar knew he was going to die. But he did not flinch away. He would not face the end as a coward.

Otec whacked at the ice shards with his cane.

Elice screamed, "I'll make a bargain!"

Ilyenna turned to face her daughter. "You are willing to strike a deal with the queen of all the winter fairies?" Adar had seen that same hungry gleam before—no fairy could resist a bargain. Especially when she knew she would win.

When Elice's eyes came to rest on him, he shook his head. He would rather have her here, making her sculptures of ice and living what life she could, than torn apart by fairy magic. "Their price is always too high."

But Elice's expression only hardened. "Yes," she said.

Adar wasn't sure if her confirmation was for him or her mother. Maybe both.

A slow, brittle smile spread across Ilyenna's face. "Very well. If you can pass beyond my queendom by the close of Winter's End, you and the boy shall go free. Fail, and you will happily return here and never again leave."

Adar could see Elice calculating in her head before she said, "Nine days. And you swear you and your fairies won't interfere or try to stop us?"

"We will not. But I warn you, Elice, my protection will be withdrawn. If you want your freedom, you must earn it alone."

"You can't trust her, Elly," Adar hissed. "She won't keep her end of the bargain—they never do."

"And if I fail," Elice went on, ignoring him, "you'll let Adar go? You won't hurt him?"

Ilyenna spread her hands and gave a little bow. "He shall be free to do as he pleases, provided he never return to the Winter Queendom."

Elice stared at the fairy who was her mother. "And the price?"

"You will lose everything save yourself."

Elice took a deep breath, then let it out. "I accept."

"Then it is done," Ilyenna's voice rang with authority. Elice winced and Adar knew what she was feeling—the bands of the bargain snapped in place tight over her ribs. He knew enough about fairies and their magic to know they were both doomed.

With a wave of Ilyenna's hand, the ice encasing Elice turned to snow. She stood on shaking legs, snow cascading from her. Head held high, she marched to Adar and pulled him up by his good hand. Pain stabbed through his shoulder, and he wobbled a little. She wrapped her arm around him and steadied him against her side.

Her grandfather was already free. He shuffled up the rise and wrapped Elice in his arms. "But that I could come with you."

Elice held on just as tightly. "You're the only person who keeps any humanity in her at all." That he would not make the journey was left unspoken, though they both had to know it was true.

Otec held her at arm's length. "I can't let you face this alone."

"I'm not alone," Elice whispered back.

After a long time, he released her and glanced at Adar, his gaze assessing. "I hold you responsible for her."

Adar knew immediately what the other man meant. "I will spare her the price, if I can." Though he knew that if they did manage to escape, Elice would pay that and more. Fire and burning, what had he done?

Elice took first one step back and then another, her gaze never leaving her grandfather's face. "I swear," he said, "one day, we will be a family again."

Elice's gaze flashed to her mother before settling back on her grandfather, and she gave him a wobbly smile. "I know."

Otec nodded and Elice turned, her tread heavy. This time, Adar took her hand, pulling her to his side. He retrieved the ice knife from where it had fallen, then tucked it back into its sheath on his belt. Together, they crested the hill and started down the other side.

12

Though it was the middle of the night, the sun still shone brightly, as it always did this time of year in the queendom. But for once, Elice was blind to the light. To her left was the sound of the rolling waves. To the right were the massive cliffs of the glacier. The vast emptiness around her felt like a living thing, sucking the life from her. She listened to the wailing call of the seals, their haunting melody making the night all the more bitter.

"You need to rest, Elice," Adar said from beside her. She heard the pain and cold in his voice—he'd hit her tree very hard. She reached out, taking his hand.

"I've already lost everything. What else does my mother think to take?"

Adar cleared his throat. "There's a story about how the stars came into the sky, it involves a woman and—"

"Luminash." Elice knew he was trying to distract her and felt infinitely grateful for it. "I read that in a book." She pushed her palms into her eyes to stave off her tears. "A book Chriel gave me." She choked back a sob. "My mother revoked her ability to transfer and killed her."

Adar gathered Elice into a one-armed hug. "Why? Because Chriel spoke of the Sundering?"

Elice nodded against his chest. "She said it was all lies told by the Summer Queen to undermine my mother."

Adar squeezed her tighter. "It's not lies. Have you ever heard about creatures of the past age?"

Elice looked up at him and sniffed. "Some. Chriel told a story of elves and dwarves and Hebocks."

"I'll tell you another, this one about mermaids, but only if you promise to lie down and get some rest. You're staggering with exhaustion."

He spread the blanket over the snow. She didn't resist as he pulled her down next to him, his hand never leaving hers. "At the end of the first age, our ancestors had fins and lived in great cities beneath the sea. Split into great queendoms, the mer still ruled the waters and all the creatures within them. They knew how to capture the magic from the world around them and shape it to their will. Because of this great magic, their cities shone with such luster and brilliance that they lit up the night sky far above them and left all the water turquoise. They mined deep within the earth, finding gemstones and gold and trading them with the dwarves on shore.

"No one knows quite how it happened, but a creature rose up—all sharp claws and terrible teeth. Its hide was tough as armor, and it had a voracious appetite for mer. At first, the mer did not fear it, sure their magic would protect them. But the magic failed, slipping away in the parting of night and morning. For months, the mer fought back with harpoon and trident, desperate to destroy the monster. But they could not kill it. Could not even harm it.

"Within a year, the greatest civilization ever known was on the brink of destruction. It was then that the mer fled the waters, washing up on the red shore and begging for aid. And there they died, for a mer cannot live long outside of the water. But they would rather face a peaceful end than a bloody one.

"Then the magic's new form appeared—an ethereal being, more spirit than creature. Magic poured from it, bleeding into everything it touched. This creature, now called a unicorn, took pity on the dying mer and changed them, replacing their gills with lungs and granting the mer enough magic to survive. In time, the mer flourished and became known as the elves of the second age."

Elice mulled over the tale. "Chriel told a story like that—it got her killed."

Adar watched her, sympathy in his gaze. "It's called the re-birth. And it's always a time of turmoil. But if you think about it, there weren't any sides between the mer queendoms anymore. It was all just about survival."

Elice rubbed her forehead. "They're just stories for children. They aren't in the history books."

Adar looked away, staring into the distance without seeming to see anything. "Who knows, maybe the mer are still there, and we just don't see them anymore."

"Are you even listening to me?"

"I like to think there is something left from the previous ages, that they aren't completely gone."

Elice let out a long sigh. He squeezed her hand and said, "Just go to sleep."

Adar bolted upright, a sharp ache cutting through him as his gaze scanned the cloud-smeared sky. He saw nothing but the huge glacier to his right, the ocean to his left, and the shore stretching on before and behind. Elice sat up beside him, wiping the sleep from her eyes. It could only have been a few hours since they lay down, for he could see the exhaustion in her bleary eyes.

"What is it?" she asked.

His every instinct was humming to life. "I don't know." He pulled out the dagger she had given him and pushed himself up with his good arm, not for the first time wishing he was whole.

Elice didn't question him, she simply shoved the blankets into the pack and wrapped them up tight. He took hold of her hand and they started moving, hurrying along the snow-packed shore. They waded across dozens of streamlets that slipped from under the iceberg like a river through a delta.

Suddenly Elice froze, pulling Adar to a halt. "There."

Ahead of them stood a pure-white bear, taller than Adar and twice as long. It was the largest bear he had ever seen. The animal blocked their way and seemed to be guarding the path.

In Elice's opposite hand, a wickedly sharp ice spear formed.

"What do we do?" Adar asked her.

"Go around. It outweighs us five to one, and it's faster."

"There is no way around." He gestured to the sheer glacier rising hundreds of feet beside them. But Elice didn't head for it, instead sidestepping toward the sea. "Elice . . . what are you doing?"

She walked onto the water, ice spreading before her feet in a long, thick path. Adar started to follow her but balked at the edge, staring down at the black waters beneath the ice. He could almost feel them closing over his head, sucking away life and heat. "This didn't work out so well for me the last time," he joked weakly.

"Adar," she said breathlessly.

He followed her gaze. More bears had joined the first, standing shoulder to shoulder in an unnaturally straight row. He squinted and saw fairies perched on the bears' shoulders. "That's cheating," he cried, outraged.

Elice's mouth was a thin line. "My mother promised she and her fairies wouldn't interfere. I guess she thinks this doesn't count."

Adar took a step out onto the ice and gestured to the cliffs. "The glacier—"

"Inland is a vast desert—there's nothing to eat." When he hesitated, she pleaded, "You have to trust me."

He readjusted his grip on the knife and hurried after Elice on the ice path, the dark ocean spreading out on both sides. The path bobbed with the waves. He glanced back and realized more bears had joined the others this time from the way they'd come. Why weren't they moving in to attack? Adar had just turned to ask Elice when he saw a flash of gray beneath them. "Elice, there's something down there."

Before she could respond, a massive form exploded from the water, huge jaws gaping at him. Adar only had time to lift his good arm to shield himself before the form rammed into him, driving him into the water and cutting off Elice's scream with the rush of water in his ears. The cold was instant, stabbing Adar to his core. He floundered in the water, not sure which way was up or down. In the rush of bubbles, he couldn't even make out what had attacked him. But he could hear it. Bird-like chirps and cricket-like trills mingled with a haunting moan.

When the bubbles cleared, he recognized the creature as a seal—pale belly and a dark-gray back sprinkled with dark spots. It was even bigger than the polar bears. And it was charging toward Adar. He considered the knife and then whirled and started to swim away, but it grabbed hold of his arm with sharp teeth, bearing down hard before dragging him to the bottom.

He struggled, but his injured arm was pinned to his side. His good arm was trapped in the monster's teeth, blood pouring from the wound. Having already used his breath to shout a warning, Adar felt his lungs screaming for air. Fire and burning, he was going to drown in the blasted ocean after all.

But then something rushed past him. The seal jerked as an ice spear impaled its back. Suddenly free, Adar swam for the surface, his movements jerky and uncoordinated because of the cold and his bandaged shoulder. Backlit by the gray sky, Elice dove toward him, her hair streaking out behind her.

He had nearly reached her when he saw movement in his peripheral vision. Dozens of seals churned in the water, each with a fairy clutching their shoulders. Wearing strange sheets of ice on her feet, Elice grabbed Adar's hand and settled it firmly on her bare shoulder. The cold stopped attacking him, but it had already done its damage, for his muscles were stiff and uncoordinated.

Dozens of icicles shot out from Elice, pulses of them— once, twice, three times, driving the seals back. She never stopped kicking upward, dragging Adar with her. As soon as they broke the surface, he gasped for air. For a moment, all he could do was breathe.

Elice let out a shrill whistle. Adar kept his gaze on the water, watching as another seal charged toward him. "Elice!"

She whipped around and launched a spear even as ice swelled under Adar, lifting him. It was thick and clear, forming a large ice floe, which he floated on like a raft. Almost immediately, it was soaked with blood from his arm. Wincing with pain, he pulled his left arm out of the sling and pressed against the puncture marks on his right arm. Fortunately it didn't seem broken.

Adar watched another seal launch itself at him from below. He cringed as it thudded into the ice. The floe jolted but didn't break. He let out the breath he'd been holding, though his body was still clenched against the bitter cold.

Elice reached up from the water. Using his bitten arm, Adar took hold of her hand to haul her onto the ice, but she pulled the cold from him first, turning the water logging his clothing into a dry snow that sifted off him. His entire body sagged in relief, though he was still shivering and his left shoulder and right arm burned. Elice had pulled herself halfway onto the ice floe when another seal darted toward her. Adar shouted a warning, but the seal had already clamped onto Elice's arm and dragged her out of sight.

Adar scrambled toward her, ready to dive back into the water, but she bobbed back to the surface. "It's all right. It's only Picca."

His gaze shifted to the seal and he recognized the animal he'd shared a cave with for several days. Elice formed a handle on the ice floe around Adar and held on while the seal dragged them both toward the shore. Elice's gaze was trained on any approaching seals, which received a stab from an ice spear for their trouble.

When the ice floe ran aground, Elice wrapped her arms around Picca's neck and kissed her. Adar didn't have time to feel relieved, for the fairies riding the bears gave a shrill war cry. The bears charged forward.

"Elice, we have to go!"

He struggled to his feet, fighting the cold that had seeped into his muscles, making him sluggish and numb. At least his arm had stopped bleeding. Elice whispered goodbye to her seal and draped Adar's good arm around her shoulder. They ran for the glacier cliffs rising before them. For the hundredth time, he wished for a fire to warm his frozen body.

They reached the base of the glacier. Elice held out her hands, ice springing from her, coating the sides in roughhewn stairs. Adar started up them, not sure how he kept his body moving. By the time they were about halfway up the cliffs, his lungs burned with every inhale, but at least he wasn't quite as cold. He chanced a glance back to see if the bears were after them and realized Elice was making the stairs crumble behind her.

While their escape had slowed the bears, it hadn't stopped them. They were scaling the cliffs, their claws digging into the packed snow. Even as Adar watched, one fell with a roar. The fairy abandoned its shoulders and zipped away.

"Elice, they're still coming!"

"Keep moving," she panted.

He finally reached the top of the cliffs, Elice right behind him. She whirled around and peered down. Grateful for the pause, Adar braced his hand on his knees, his breath sawing in and out of his lungs. In the distance, a pod of orca feasted on the carcasses of the dead seals.

Elice raised her hands. The glacier beneath the bears began to crumble, sending bears careening toward the shore.

"Take that, you overgrown goats!" Adar tried to shout in triumph, but the frigid air seared his lungs and left him coughing, ruining the effect. But then snow shot up from the shore, cushioning the bears' fall and steadily growing under them to push them closer to their targets.

Adar pointed. "That's cheating!"

Elice tipped her head toward the poisonous green sky. "Mother," she screamed. "You swore you would not harm us."

"I swore that neither I nor my fairies would harm him," came Ilyenna's disembodied voice, her body having lost its physical form. "But I made no promise about the creatures of my realm."

"Still cheating!" Adar shouted back in disgust.

Elice backed away from the cliff face, snatching Adar's hand and pulling him with her. "We have to run."

They took off across the frozen expanse, Elice spanning the numerous ravines with bridges of ice. Adar glanced over his shoulder as the first of the bears crested the glacier, legs churning. In only a few strides, the bears were catching up, surrounding Adar and Elice. And all of the creatures, fairies and bears alike, had their gazes pinned hungrily on him.

He heard their panting and whipped around in time to see a bear moving to cut them off, so close he could make out shredded flesh between the animal's teeth. Adar held out his dagger. "Elice," he warned.

But she had already stuttered to a halt. He slammed into her, and they both went down and then scrambled to their feet. She tried to pull him behind her, but they were surrounded, so there was no "behind." Slavering, the bears prowled around them, the only sound their huge paws scraping along the snow.

"Well," Adar said through clenched teeth. "I can honestly say I'd rather drown than be eaten alive. Can we go back to the ocean?"

"Stay out of the way, daughter of winter, and you will not be harmed," said one of the fairies from atop the shoulders of a bear.

Elice took a step back from the fairy who had spoken. "Mother! You cannot kill him! You promised!"

"I won't kill him. Just maim a little. He'll still be perfectly alive."

"Give me one of your spears," Adar said. He might not be able to fight off a dozen polar bears, but he could do a little maiming of his own.

Elice set her teeth, defiance sparking in her honey eyes. "You're not going to hurt him." To Adar, she said, "Sheath that dagger." He opened his mouth to question her when he felt the ice beneath his feet began to crack. He looked down as the opaque ice thinned. Below them, he could make out a brilliant blue ravine that darkened to black. He shoved the dagger in its sheath. "Elly, I don't think this is a good idea."

"Better than being eaten," she reminded him. And then they were falling.

13

Elice plummeted, arms windmilling. Concentrating, she managed to form an ice slide beneath her. She and Adar landed on it, morphing their freefall into a skidding, spilling plunge that carried them at an angle toward the bottom of the fissure.

Before Elice could react, the fissure narrowed. She tried to duck, but her head smacked into a shelf of ice. Sparks of black blossomed in her vision, and her body felt numb and far away. Adar's hand grabbed her, his legs wrapping around her torso.

Then the ice slide disappeared beneath them and they were freefalling again.

"Elice!" he yelled. She shook herself, seeing the churning river rising up toward them. She pulled on winter, barely managing to encase them in a pod of ice before they plunged into the water.

Sprawled on top of Adar, she waited to see if the ice would hold. It shivered but stayed together. She pulled more magic, reinforcing and thickening it as they careened along an enormous river beneath the glacier. Through the clear ice, she could make out a narrow ravine twisting above them, a chaotic river flowing through the center of it.

He relaxed his death grip on her. "Definitely better than being eaten by a bear." He looked into Elice's eyes. "You all right?"

She gently probed the growing knot on her forehead. Her first attempt at speaking came out garbled. She rolled her tongue around, smacked her lips, and tried again. "I think so. You?"

He shot her his cocky grin. "I'm trapped with a beautiful girl lying on top of me—do you even have to ask?"

Despite herself, she chuckled. "You're incorrigible."

He brushed a finger down her cheek. "And someday you're going to fall madly in love with me for it."

She was suddenly aware of how close they were, his body pressed against hers. She could feel his heart beating through their clothes. "Don't count on it."

He chuckled. "Always the doubter."

The pod hit something. Elice braced herself to keep from being thrown around. Their pace picked up, and another bump jostled them. It suddenly got very dark. She sensed the water all around them—they were in some kind of tunnel.

"How much air do we have?" Adar's voice came from the pitch black.

She'd never tested an air bubble this large. "No more talking," she told him. The pod slammed into something, sending them spinning end over end.

They braced themselves against the wall of the pod and managed to ride through the worst of it. But they had another problem, more immediate, if less pressing than their diminishing air. "Adar . . ." Elice said very carefully. Before he could respond, she threw up all over him.

He made a sound that was half surprise and half disgust. There was a sudden light, but before Elice could get her bearings, they were plunging down so fast she could only scream. They hit water and sank slowly before floating back to the surface. Behind them and to Elice's right, a roaring waterfall crashed into a clear pool, which must have been where they had fallen from. Far above was a sliver of daylight that sent a brilliant shaft of light streaming down into a narrow, jade-colored cavern that emptied into another black tunnel.

She reached for Adar's hand. "Don't let go."

"I won't."

She dissipated the pod, and they both went under the surface of the water. Adar was true to his word, holding tightly to her hand so she could keep the cold at bay. Together, they kicked to the surface. The current pulled them relentlessly toward the tunnel.

"I'm thinking we don't want to do that again," Adar commented dryly. Still holding hands, they kicked for a shelf of ice. When Elice could feel slush beneath her, she hauled herself up, Adar helping her keep her balance. They waded onto a slippery ice shelf. Elice turned the water on their bodies to snow, and they brushed each other off.

Adar flopped down, pulling her down with him. He scooted his back against the glacier. Somewhere along the way, he had lost his hat. "Your mother really needs to work on her diplomacy. Also, keeping her promises."

She noticed blood soaking through his sleeve and motioned toward his forearm. "How bad is it?"

He shrugged. "I've had worse."

"I remember." She helped him out of his torn coat and rolled up his bloody sleeve to reveal teeth marks. Elice pulled one apart to gauge its depth as he hissed through his teeth. "I don't see any torn muscle, which is a relief," she said. "But you could use a few stitches."

"Shall we ask your mother to fetch your supplies from the cave?"

Ignoring his comment, Elice took his dagger and cut a strip from her hem before handing back the knife. She bandaged Adar's wound and rewrapped his sling, which had come loose at some point. "You know, I've lost a lot of clothes because of you," she told him.

"This coming from the woman who left my clothes on the bottom of the ocean. Also, you vomited on me. I can still smell it," he said, his tone light.

Blushing, Elice sat back and looked up at the pale light filtering in from above. They were in a narrow crevice in the ice. The walls had been carved by the ebb and flow of flood water, revealing subtle bands that varied from pale mint to deep jade that formed curving outcroppings of rock in fantastical patterns.

"This reminds me of home," Adar said.

Elice turned to him. "It does?"

"I grew up in caves that opened up to narrow fissures of red rock. In the wider fissures, we planted crops along the basins, watering them from irrigation we took from the subterranean lakes."

She sighed as she looked around. "It's actually kind of beautiful."

"Elly, please, this is no time to be flirting with me."

"You always manage to twist my words."

"You like it. Don't bother denying it." She *was* actually starting to like it. But if he knew that, he'd become insufferable. "How are we going to get out of here?"

She glanced far above them. "We could climb out."

"Back up to the bears?" Adar sniffed. "Besides, fairies hate being underground. We're safer down here."

"Good point." Elice nodded to the tunnel where the river disappeared. "We could try that again."

"I'd rather not be thrown up on again." He looked toward the second, higher tunnel. "What about that one?"

They trudged to their feet, scaled the sloping wall, and peered down the darkened tunnel. It was narrow at the top and bottom and wider at the sides, which were slick and shiny.

Elice swallowed nervously. "Think it will take us where we need to go?"

"I bet in the summer, this whole cavern is full of water and this is another river. All rivers lead to the ocean, which is generally south. If the sun crossed the sky like it's supposed to, I could figure out if we were going east or west. But here it just does useless circles around the horizon."

Elice thought for a moment. East would lead them back to the palace. They needed to head southwest. "All this water has to come out somewhere. If it came out to the east, we would have crossed a river before we fell into the glacier."

Adar smiled. "Well then, onward, my good woman."

She laid down a path of snow to even out the bottom of the uneven tunnel, and they stepped inside. It wasn't long before the tunnel grew pitch black, and even with Elice forming a perfectly smooth path, her steps were halting and unsure. Adar seamlessly took the lead, which helped, but only a little.

"Elice," he finally said. "What's wrong?"

She used her free hand to wipe away the sweat on her brow. "Nothing."

"It's not nothing," he growled. "Your hand is all sweaty, which is ludicrous considering how cold it is, and you're shaking."

She let out a shuddering breath. "I—I'm afraid of the dark." She bumped into Adar before she noticed he'd stopped.

"But . . . don't you live in complete darkness for two months out of the year?"

She nodded before realizing he couldn't see her. "Yes. But my mother always leaves an aurora in the sky so I'm not afraid."

He let out a long breath. "You have no idea how much I want to help you with that."

Why did he sound so sad? "There's nothing you can do. Nothing either of us can do but keep walking." She suddenly wished she was as strong as her mother, for then she could call on her own aurora to light their way. But then she had a sudden memory. When Chriel died, Elice had been so furious she'd forgotten that her mother was stronger. At that moment, Elice had pulled from winter harder than ever. And she'd managed to dissipate her mother's ice faster than Ilyenna could make it.

"What if I could make an aurora?" she said quietly, almost to herself.

"What?"

She licked her lips. "I want to try something."

"Well, we are running for our lives, but if you want to kiss me, I can't see denying you."

She threw a glare his way.

"Did you glare at me?" Adar laughed. "'Cause I *swear* I felt it, and I'd hate to miss one of your glares. You get this line between your eyes, and your nose wrinkles up. It's adorable."

Elice smacked him. "Be quiet. I've never tried this before."

She closed her eyes and concentrated, pulling light and color from winter in ways she never had before. When she opened her eyes, the weird green lights of the aurora, tinged in purple, shimmered like ribbons above them. The light was faint, but it chased away the all-encompassing shadows.

"I did it!" She grinned in relief. She glanced up at Adar, but his gaze was fixed on the aurora, his mouth gaping. Something soft opened up inside her at the wonder in his expression.

Slowly, he turned to look down at her. "Sometimes, I wish you weren't so amazing, Elice."

She blinked. "What?"

He shook his head, the wonder in his eyes shuttered away. "Never mind. Let's keep going."

They walked on for what must have been miles, but Elice's hard-packed snow made their steps sure, so they made good time.

The tunnel gradually lightened and widened, circling away from them in ever-widening arches until they stepped into a cavern. Elice enlarged her aurora, illuminating a hundred thousand icicles that dripped from the ceiling and every outcropping. They made the walls look as if they were made up of thousands of columns.

Some of the larger icicles in the ceiling had trickled water onto the floor, which had refrozen until it formed a mirror image. As Elice and Adar went on, some of these twin icicles met at a delicate point, creating hourglass shapes. Those shapes eventually fused into broad columns until it appeared that the travelers were wandering through a vast cathedral.

"Fire and burning," Adar breathed out. "It's like a temple of ice."

"Fire and burning. You've said that before." Elice turned to him with a quizzical look. "I thought it was an Idaran expression."

He harrumphed. "Tribesmen were saying it long before Idarans."

They couldn't be sure how long they had traveled underground, but they were both exhausted. They spent a night in the cathedral of ice, the aurora shifting above them. The next morning, they passed into another tunnel, ducking beneath icicles hanging from the rim like daggers. Here, light filtered in from outside, the walls glowing a deep mint. They walked for hours before the tunnel opened up again.

Here, it was dimmer and colder. The walls were lined with bright-blue ice, water flowing through veins in the snow before freezing again. The resulting pattern reminded Elice of the vast roots of a tree. Eventually, those veins opened up, a thousand small waterfalls running through and down the walls, making the snow slushy. Puddles began to form. Those puddles met and merged into a vast mint-green lake, the surface a perfect reflection of the ceiling, which looked like rolling, puffy storm clouds frozen in place.

Elice and Adar crossed the surface of the lake on a floating bridge of packed snow. The lake was so clear and perfect, Elice couldn't help but take a long drink that tasted of minerals and snow. But her stomached ached with hunger—she and Adar hadn't eaten anything since the morning before.

Though it was beautiful here, and safe, Elice knew they had to get out. So when the lake ended in a gentle river, they didn't even discuss it. She made them another pod, this one a bit bigger than the last, and they climbed inside, curled around each other, and fell asleep to the gentle rocking.

14

Adar woke when he couldn't fight off the pain any longer. His shoulder was an old throb he'd become somewhat used to, but his arm burned fresh and bright. And deeper still, a familiar ache, a spreading heat that felt cold. He was fevering, and without Elice's touch, he knew the bitter cold would be unbearable. She was curled against his side, her right arm and leg thrown over him, her cheek pressed into his chest. Even in her sleep, she kept the aurora bright above them.

He lay perfectly still, enjoying the weight of her body. Her breathing was rhythmic and deep, her face soft and open. This was the girl he'd known for only six days. A girl of contradictions, for she was innocent and tough, young and old, delicate and strong. He never would have defied a queen, not the way Elice had. More than anything, he felt a protectiveness well up within him, which was ridiculous. Here, she had all the power. And with his damaged shoulder, Adar couldn't even fight off a drunk.

If he was honest with himself, the biggest threat she faced was him. He knew he shouldn't want to hold her like this, shouldn't feel this way at all—especially not about *her*. And he *would* stop enjoying himself. Eventually.

But then the blasted river began tossing them about. He wrapped his arms around her, not because he wanted to hold her—he was just trying to keep her from being jostled. And then they plunged down and popped up again. Elice's eyes flew open and she reared back, smacking her head on the top of the pod with a crack. Her face screwed up, and she hissed through her teeth.

Adar's arms felt strangely empty without her. "You really should be careful with your head. You only have the one, you know."

She opened an eye to peer down at her body, which was spread along the length of his. She met his gaze, her face mottled with mortification, which made her even more adorable. She scrambled off him. "Sorry!"

Adar stretched his sore muscles. "Even in your sleep, you can't resist me."

She smacked him on the chest, his sickness making it hurt more than it should have. Not that he'd ever let on. She squinted a little and the aurora grew stronger, its beauty taking his breath away. "I think we're going to make—"

The pod slammed into the river bottom so hard the ice shattered completely. Elice's hand was ripped from Adar's. The cold knifed into him so hard he sucked in a breath of water in shock.

Elice fought against the current—tried to swim—but the river spun her about like a too-eager child with a toy. She started to form an ice floe to lift her to the surface. The ice slammed into something, forcing her breath from her and sending her reeling. She gasped without meaning to, and water invaded her lungs. Then her muscles lost all their strength and she careened along helplessly. All she could think was that she'd failed Adar and proven her mother right. The blackness took her.

She was aware of something snagging on her belt, her body being pulled against the current. And then Elice felt hands on her, hauling her to the slushy shore. Those hands lifted her into a sitting position. "Breathe!" came a voice.

But she couldn't breathe. She was dying. A hand came down hard on her back and she suddenly remembered how to cough. Water spewed from her mouth. A ragged, gurgling breath. Then she coughed more water. It was agony, breathing air and coughing water. But eventually her gasps slowed and her vision cleared.

There were three of them, all with dark skin and features. The girl who had pounded Elice's back, an older man with a wispy mustache that fluttered all the way down to his chest, and another man with a large mole over his left eye. The two men were loading Adar's shivering body onto a sled pulled by a dozen large dogs. Beside the sled was the carcass of a seal.

Adar turned his head and met Elice's gaze with obvious relief.

The girl who'd helped Elice breathe was probably around her own age and was buried in furs so only her round face showed. She was dark-skinned, like Adar, but her features were round and her eyes almond-shaped. The girl draped Elice's arm over her shoulder and helped her toward one of the sleds. But Elice's legs weren't working properly, and she promptly fell down again.

The mustached man ran back to them and lifted Elice in his arms, then deposited her on the sled. "Mush," they cried to their dogs. The sleds moved out with a little jerk and steadily picked up speed as the dogs strained against their harnesses. Still dazed, Elice shifted to look at Adar. He was shivering so hard he seemed to be convulsing.

"We have to stop." she said. "I have to help him."

The girl didn't seem to understand her but shouted over the wind, "Our hut is just there. It's warm." It was then Elice realized the girl wasn't speaking Clannish, but Svass. Since the Winter Queendom was at the heart of Svassheim, Elice's father had insisted she learn the language.

Elice peered ahead and saw a hut built in an alcove along the shore. Strung out on lengthy poles all along it were about a dozen seal carcasses in various stages of being butchered. These were highmen, she realized—the Svass who lived inside the Winter Queendom. How far had she and Adar come from the Winter Palace?

The sleds eased to a stop, and the two men hauled Adar inside the hut. With the girl's help, Elice managed to stand up and follow after them. Inside the smoky, dark shelter, the fire had burned low, but it was warm—warmer than Elice's cave had ever been. More warmth than she ever remembered feeling.

The men immediately set about pulling off Adar's clothes, while the girl dumped more of what looked like dung onto the fire. Once he was stripped to the skin, they piled furs on top of him, but he was shivering so hard they kept slipping off.

The girl set some kind of cookware directly on the fire and then came to Elice. "Your clothes are frozen solid."

Without thinking, Elice thawed them. The girl's mouth came open. "Winter Queen."

The men eased to their feet and moved toward the door. "Sakari," said the one with the mustache, motioning for the girl to come with him.

Elice wasn't surprised by the fear in their eyes—she should have been more careful. She held her hands up, trying to appear harmless. "No. I'm not the Winter Queen. I'm her daughter, Elice. We're trying to escape."

"Sometimes, Elice, you want to keep your next play hidden," Adar said through chattering teeth.

"You speak Svass?" she shot at him.

"Grew up in a library, remember?"

"The river spewed you from the glacier," growled the mustached man.

"Please, we need help," Elice said.

The men hesitated, sharing a long look. "How can we help you?" the mole man asked warily.

Elice pointed to Adar. "He needs to be warm. I can keep the cold from him, but I cannot keep him warm." She dropped her head, ashamed at how often she had failed him. "And we're hungry. We haven't eaten in over two days."

Silent communication passed between the two men. The quiet one nodded. The mustached man squatted and looked at them. "I am Anuniaq, this is my brother, Kiviuq, and that is our niece, Sakari. We will give you food and shelter, but tomorrow you must move on, for we will not risk the wrath of the Winter Queen."

Elice let out a grateful sigh. "Thank you." She returned her attention to Adar. "How's the bite? You seem to be favoring your right arm."

He studied her for a moment, his expression indecisive. "I'm more concerned about the hat I lost. I loved that hat." Knowing he was trying to distract her, she shot him a stern look. With a grump, he obediently held out his right arm. Elice unwrapped the dirty bandage as carefully as she could, but Adar still winced and gasped a bit. When she reached his bare arm, Elice was alarmed to see the puncture wounds were swollen and red. They smelled bad, too.

She fought down her panic. "Can you bring me some saltwater?" she asked Sakari, who quietly slipped outside. Her passing let in a burst of cold air that made Adar cringe.

"I should have thought to bring some medicines," Elice murmured. "I'm sorry."

Adar's eyes were closed, his face red. "We were sort of in a hurry."

"I'm going to help your body flush out the infection, but it's going to hurt," she warned.

Anuniaq handed Adar a bit of bone to bite down on. Sakari returned with some seawater in a bowl carved out of bone.

"Get it hot," Elice told her.

"I have some medicines I can put in it," Sakari said softly. "It will help with the swelling."

Elice nodded. When it was just short of boiling, she poured the water, floating with some crushed seaweed, back into the bowl. "Rest your arm in there," she ordered. Adar did, wincing as his wound seemed to swell even more. When his skin was hot to the touch, she lifted his arm from the water and stretched it out straight.

"Hold him like this," Elice said to the men. They held his arm while she rubbed toward the open wounds. Watery pus squirted out, and she rubbed again as it oozed and then clear flu-id ran down. Adar hissed through his teeth, his whole body locking up and the cords of muscle and sinew standing out in his dark skin. Elice tried to think only about clearing the wounds, not about the pain she was causing him. When she was done, she cleaned the puncture marks with the water from the bowl.

"No need to wrap it just yet," she said, her hands shaking only a little. "Best to let it breathe."

Adar cradled his arm to his body. Elice reached forward, laying her fingertips gently on his arm and letting just a trickle of cold spread into his arm, until some of the redness and puffiness eased.

"It's sore, but it actually feels better," he said in relief.

"You should have told me how bad it was." She was hurt that he hadn't. "Now, let's take a look at your shoulder." She unwrapped it and was pleased to see the dark bruises had faded to a sickly green. "You should move it and stretch it every day now. But if there's any chance you might get hurt, you should keep it in the sling."

"So, it should pretty much always stay in the sling," he joked.

She smiled at him, realizing he not only joked around when he was trying to lighten the mood, but also when he was afraid. She started rubbing his shoulder to get the muscles to loosen up. Adar grimaced and gave a little groan. "The accident you mentioned, where you got these scars—what happened?" Elice asked him

"Let's just say it involved a chariot race and a bet I didn't win." He lifted his arm and tested its motion, then smiled with what she hoped was gratitude.

Sakari passed Elice a bone cup of something brown and steaming. "Moss tea," the girl said. Elice tipped it up and took a swallow, choking as it scalded her mouth. They all stared at her in confusion. Embarrassed, she let her mouth flood with cold to sooth the burn.

"You have to blow across the top to cool it," Adar said as he cupped the liquid with his left hand, letting the steam rise to his face.

Not wanting to repeat the experience, Elice set the cup down. Sakari, who was laying out Adar's clothes to dry, gasped when she saw the dagger. Elice reached over, took her father's belt, and settled it beside Adar. "It won't hurt you."

Sakari eyed the fire. "Won't it melt?"

"No," Elice said simply. "Where are we?" she asked the highmen.

Kiviuq used the knife in his hand to point west. "Two days by dogsled to my village."

"How many days until we leave the Winter Queendom?"

Kiviuq tipped his head to the side. "I do not understand."

"A place where ice melts completely from the ground, plants grow, and animals can live off the land and not just the sea."

Kiviuq stared at her. "I have heard of such a place. It is very far south, farther than I have ever been." He stepped back. "We must finish butchering the meat before it freezes. Rest here." The two men stepped back outside, Sakari reluctantly following them.

As soon as they were gone, Elice looked at Adar in concern. They'd only left the palace a few days ago, and she couldn't be sure how long they'd spent inside the glacier—a couple of days, maybe. Already he had been dangerously close to dying three times.

She scooted closer to Adar, whose hands were shaking too much to drink his tea. She took it from him and held it to his lips. "I'm sorry."

He swallowed. "What for?"

"I couldn't keep the ice from breaking. I—"

"Ice is brittle, Elice. You can't change the nature of that."

"But I should have made it thicker. I should have been faster."

He grinned at her over the rim of the cup. "Look at the bright side. Nothing tried to eat us."

She closed her eyes. In her world, he was so fragile, so easily broken. How was she going to keep him alive for however much farther they had to go? "If I went back to my mother now, she'd let you go. You would be safe with these people. They can help you get out of the queendom."

Adar leaned in to her and whispered, "Elice, your mother has already proven she's willing to break her promises. I'm safer with you than not, believe me. Besides, I can't leave you pining away after me in that palace for the rest of your life—you'd make a terrible piner."

Elice choked on a drink of tea. "I would not!"

His eyes twinkled. "There's the fire."

So many retorts filled Elice's mind that she couldn't pick just one. She nearly glared at him before remembering that he *liked* it when she glared at him.

Adar laughed outright. "You really are the best person I've ever teased—including my sisters. And I have seven of them."

Elice let out a long-suffering sigh. "I don't know why I ever considered you a friend."

He gave her an exaggerated frown. "Just a friend? I thought we were past that."

She was saved from having to respond when Sakari came back inside with strips of blubber and skin in her hands.

"What is it?" Elice asked.

"Narwhal." Sakari poured liquid from a water skin into cups. "My uncles bring you blood to make you strong, and blubber to keep you warm."

"Wonderful," Adar said, his face a little green. But he drank the blood and ate the blubber without complaint. Elice cut off a piece for herself and chewed and chewed and chewed, then sipped at the blood.

Sakari watched them for a few minutes, then said, "If you go south, I will come with you."

Elice stopped chewing. She and Adar exchanged a dubious glance. "Why?"

Sakari stared at them, unflinching. "I would leave the forever ice."

Elice didn't know what to say, or how to react. It was Adar who cleared his throat and said, "What about your uncles? Surely they won't want you to leave them."

Sakari blinked slowly, as if just waking up. "It is not their decision to make. Besides, my mother's family is from the south, a village that grows in the forests. They are reindeer herders. We lived with them when I was a girl. I will go back to them."

"It wouldn't be safe for you," Elice said gently. "My mother hunts us."

Sakari gazed into the embers. "This winter, we hunted the narwhals on the edge of the ice. The ice shook beneath us and cracked, splitting and breaking up. My father stood watch at the edge and fell into the water. I used my harpoon to pull him out. But he was already dead. I turned back to find my mother, but she was gone, fallen between the cracks in the ice. I floated for many days, thinking I would die with them. But my ice floe reached the shore.

"When I returned home, my two younger brothers and I moved in with my aunts, who cared for us as they always had. Very few men returned from hunting on the ice. The man I was to marry and another of my uncles were among those who did not come back. Then followed a very bad winter. There was no food to eat. My brothers starved. Many of the children starved." Sakari's voice was hollow.

"In the darkness, an earth tremor shook our tents, ripping apart the skins. My brothers froze to death." Her voice trailed off. "I am not afraid of the Winter Queen, for she cannot hurt one who is dead already." Sakari's dark eyes glittered. She rose to her feet and slipped back outside without a word.

Elice stared after her long after she'd left. She recognized the haunted look in her eyes—Sakari blamed herself for the deaths of those she loved. And she felt guilty for surviving when those she loved had not. Elice understood Sakari's pain all too well.

Hours later, the three Svass came back inside the tent, their hands chapped and covered in blood. "We have loaded the meat onto the sleds. We will take it back to our village. Sakari tells us she will go with you."

Elice waited for the men to forbid their niece to go, or at least try to talk her out of it. But instead, Kiviuq squatted down and pulled back the furs on the ground to reveal the packed snow beneath them. He drew his knife and traced a long curve that plunged downward. He tapped the top of the crescent. "This is where we are." He drew the knife until he reached the point where the crescent straightened into a long dive. "Here is a village of highmen. We trade with them for caribou hides—warmer than seal. So they should know a place where animals live off the land. That is all I know."

Elice recognized the drawing from the atlas back home.

"How long will it take to reach the village?" Adar asked Kuviuq.

Kuviuq stroked his scraggly mustache. "Many weeks."

Elice calculated in her head. They'd spent maybe two days in the glacier, making it about seven days since Winter's End began. "We only have seven more days to reach the Summer Realm," she said to Adar.

His brow furrowed as he studied the map carved into the packed snow. "We'll have to go by sea."

"We can't risk the open ocean again," she told him. "It's too dangerous."

Adar shook his head. "Ilyenna doesn't know where we are. If she did, she would have attacked us by now. The longer the journey takes, the more chances she has to find us. And we don't have weeks. We have days."

Elice looked into his eyes. "It's too hard to protect you over the water. And besides, we don't have a boat."

"You could make one," he said with a confidence she didn't feel.

She rubbed her forehead. "Which she'll easily spot. If she finds us out on open waters, it's over."

"So disguise it," he suggested. "If you can make something as grand as the Winter Palace, you can manage this."

"I'm not sure . . ."

"Your magic is capable, Elice. *You* are capable of more than you know. Remember the aurora?"

She stared into his eyes, seeing nothing but faith in her. "I'll try."

"And I will guide you," Sakari put in.

Kiviuq studied his dead-eyed niece. "Yesterday is ashes, tomorrow is wood. Only today does the fire shine brightly."

"I choke on ashes, Uncle," Sakari rasped.

Kiviuq let out a long breath. "When the fire burns bright in you again, perhaps you will come back to us."

She looked away. "Perhaps."

They shared another meal of meat and blood, and Adar had the intelligence not to complain once. Kiviuq and Anuniaq had brought him thick clothing made of brown fur and showed him how to put it on over the linen clothing he already wore. The first layer went fur side in, the second fur side out.

Elice watched silently. When they were finished, the highmen broke off to talk between themselves. Sakari sat quietly beside them. Adar leaned into Elice and whispered, "The fairies are looking for two people, not three. Fairies are terrible at telling people apart. Having Sakari come with us might work to our advantage."

Elice watched the girl, knowing her calm exterior hid a raging blizzard inside her. Adar yawned hugely. "Get some sleep," Elice told him with a smile.

He curled up in some furs, his face red with heat. Though Elice was exhausted, she slipped outside and crossed the waters on an icy path. When she was certain the ocean was deep enough, she held her hands out to her sides and pulled more winter than she had ever pulled before.

15

After huddling so close to the fire his cheeks burned, Adar was loath to step back into the cold. He braced himself and left the warm hut after Elice and Sakari. To his surprise, the clothing he wore shielded him from the brunt of it. Only his face stung, the bitter breeze blowing off the ocean making his cheeks burn in a different way.

He struggled to keep up, to make his steps even. His body still felt sluggish and weak, and the pain in his arm pulsed with each heartbeat. His injured shoulder ached, but he was determined not to let the discomfort show. Elice had cleaned the bite marks, but he could tell from the look on her face that she knew it was infected. The girl, Sakari, had given him something she said would ease the pain. So far it wasn't working.

Just behind Sakari, Adar paused on the shore as another path of ice spread out before them, thicker and wider than the last one. Elice must have figured out how deadly a spill into the water could be for him. "We're not walking across the ocean, right?" he teased her. "'Cause that didn't work out so well last time."

Elice cast him a look that said she knew exactly what his banter was trying to conceal—his fear. "I thought you trusted me." She posed it like a challenge.

"I trust you," he muttered. "It's your mother I'm worried about." Still, when she said it like that. He took a deep breath and tried to pretend the icy path was paving stones. When that didn't work, he simply wiped at the sweat freezing on his brow and put one foot in front of the other.

They strode toward a massive iceberg, as big as some of the mountains Adar had seen in the Highlands. It wasn't long before he realized that was where they were heading. He narrowed his gaze—there was a dark hole in the side of the iceberg. As they came closer, he realized the hole was an opening, just large enough for him to fit through. They stepped off an ice floe and onto the iceberg. He might have felt relief, except the iceberg was an awful lot like a ship. That hadn't worked out so well for him.

Elice paused before the opening and motioned for Adar and Sakari to go ahead of her. "It's bigger inside. And we'll be hidden from view."

Sakari didn't hesitate before slipping out of sight. Adar followed her, but turned when he noticed Elice had paused just past the entrance. "What are you doing?"

Elice stood with her back to him and sealed off the entrance to the iceberg with a thick layer of snow. "I anchored it to the sea floor. I have to free it." The iceberg suddenly wrenched.

Adar's gloved hand shot out, gouging out packed snow and making his arm sting. Memories of the sinking ship swamped him. He'd been climbing the rigging when the horde of ice fairies had circled the ship once, twice, three times. Behind him, the captain had started shouting, calling for the ship to turn. Adar's gaze had shifted from the fairies to the water. A long, thin dagger of ice shot out from the iceberg and plunged into the starboard side of their ship, wrenching the craft hard. A tearing sound vibrated through boards as men spilled off the icy decks and into the black water.

Adar had slammed into a mast and lost his hold. He free fell, hands scrambling at the ropes, black water rising up to meet him. And then he'd felt a rope slide through his palm. His hand fisted around it, jerking him to a stop. He'd felt a pop in his shoulder and a moment of bright pain. For an unending moment, he struggled to hold on, to grip the rope with his other hand as his feet dangled over the dark water that swallowed his shipmates, drowning out their screams as their heavy clothing pulled them down. Their faces upturned, eyes meeting his from beneath the water.

And then his fingers had opened of their own accord. He was falling toward the ocean when the ship shifted underneath him. He hit the deck hard, his head slamming into a barrel. He'd collapsed on his side. For a time, sound had gone. There was only the vibration of running feet, and then water washing over the deck. The moment it touched him, he had gasped in shock. His body and mind were still sluggish. He couldn't run. Couldn't call for help—not that there was any to be had.

He'd done the only thing he could—wrap his arm around a bit of rope dangling from the same barrel he'd hit his head on and hang on as the ship sucked him down.

Suddenly, the same face he'd seen when he'd surfaced was looking at him, though her expression was more concerned than desperate. "Adar? What's wrong?"

He shook himself, trying to find the joke that would let him forget, let him pretend all was well, but all he could find was the feel of the ship shuddering in her death throes, see the faces of his shipmates begging for help as they'd been sucked into the black abyss, feel the cold cutting into him.

Elice's arms wrapped around him, holding him together. "I can't promise it'll be all right. But I'm here," she said softly.

Above them, the aurora appeared, a pure white that made her dark hair gleam.

Adar was not alone. And if he did die in this forsaken place, at least one person would mourn him. He felt his muscles unlock one by one. Then he let out a long breath and held her too, because maybe she needed to know she wasn't alone either.

With a deep breath, she pulled back and rested her palms against his cheeks, which burned with fever and cold and now for another reason entirely. How could her cold hands spread a fire through him? Fire and burning, he wanted to touch her. Kiss her. Hold her in a way that spoke of more than comfort and friendship.

He felt the cold slinking back, held at bay by her gentle hands. And with the cold went the last of the horror. Elice stood on tiptoe, tipped his head down, and pressed her soft lips against his forehead. The act stunned him. He wanted to take her face in his hands and kiss her. But she was not his to touch. She never would be.

"You're still fevering," she said matter-of-factly. She took hold of his hand and pulled him deeper into the glacier. He went willingly—he'd follow her anywhere. "Below sea level, I shaped the glacier like a paddle to catch the currents. The top is shaped like a sail to catch the wind."

The tunnel widened into a cavern. Sakari was waiting for them, her face devoid of any of the wonder she should have felt at the shifting rivers of pastel light above them. Elice looked at the girl with the same expression on her face as when she saw a wounded animal: a single-mindedness that said she was going to heal the creature whether it liked it or not.

Adar almost felt sorry for the girl. Elice's healing was always painful.

Elice eased him down and helped him out of his layers of fur to expose his injuries. They didn't have a fire or any way to make one, so she simply rubbed his arm. There was less pus than the day before, which he thought a good sign. At least the tight throbbing eased a little. Her touch was cool, and the coolness spread. She left his arm open to the air—with her touching him, he didn't really need all the layers anyway—and hummed something tunelessly. But Adar felt himself drawn toward the sound, toward this girl of color and light. He rested his head on her thigh and fell asleep.

16

A dar watched as Elice reappeared into the cavern, brushing snow from the front of her tunic. With all her layers of fur, Sakari looked positively fluffy beside her. "We're making good time," Elice began. "Better than I thought. Sakari says the trouble we'll have is convincing the villagers to loan us their dogs."

"How long have I been asleep?" Adar asked.

Elice shared a look of concern with Sakari and hurried over to him. "Hours."

Adar winced as he sat up, his body aching deep in his bones. "Can't we buy them?" At Elice's look of confusion, he added, "The dogs?"

"You don't have anything the villagers want," Sakari answered.

Elice took some meat out of a pack, thawed it, and set it before Adar. Just looking at it made him want to gag. Even the smell . . . he felt bile rising in his throat and looked away. Elice checked his arm, seeming relieved when no more pus leaked out, only clear fluid. She massaged his shoulder, and he winced and grimaced as he worked it in circles and up and down.

When Elice was satisfied, she flooded his shoulder and arm with cold. He sighed in relief and asked, "Can we look out?"

"See for yourself," Elice said. He let her help him up, surprised by how weak he was. "Are you coming, Sakari?"

The girl settled down on some of her furs. "I will rest."

Elice narrowed her gaze and opened her mouth to say something before seeming to think better of it. She and Adar climbed up a corridor, and he had to stop often to catch his breath. At the end of the corridor, she had made an opening near the top of the glacier—a shelf just high enough for them to crawl through. It was wide enough for three people to lie side by side.

In the distance, Adar caught sight of a fleet of icebergs and ice floes. A massive iceberg jutted out like a cliff. One side of it extended out into the water, which had carved a delicate arch large enough for a ship to pass beneath. Their iceberg seemed to be moving faster than the ones around them, leaving the others behind as they pushed past.

"Adar, I'm frightened," Elice said.

He studied a small iceberg that came into view. It was black as onyx, with brilliant aqua bands gleaming in stark contrast. "We're going to make it, Elly."

"It's not that. I'm worried because I don't know how to help you. I don't have my medicines."

He removed his mitten and took her hand in his. Immediately, he felt the cold backing away. They floated past another iceberg. It looked like a misshapen head atop a thin neck. If Adar turned his head to the side and squinted, he could almost make out eyes and a mouth. He wondered how long before the head toppled off completely.

"I told you, I'm pretty hard to kill," he said teasingly.

Elice eyed him. "The scars on your body? You said something about a chariot race."

He wished she'd forgotten about that. "Next time I'm muttering while in pain or near unconscious, gag me." She gave him a look. "Some other boys were saying some pretty awful things about one of the girls at the temple," Adar explained. "She has certain . . . deformities. I wanted to hurt them—teach them a lesson. So I challenged them to a chariot race."

When he didn't immediately continue, Elice gestured for him to go on. He sighed. "They cheated, cut the straps of my harness. The chariot flipped. One of the wheels broke, and the spoke stabbed into my side. I would have died, but my mother was nearby and managed to save me."

Elice's mouth came open. "And the other men?"

Adar grinned. "They didn't win either."

"I don't understand."

"They had a problem with their axel."

"But how could you do anything to their axel? Hadn't you already crashed?"

"Let's just say I have a really good aim."

She opened her mouth to ask more questions, but he held out his hand. It was time to change the subject. "You know I'm too sick to run," he said evenly. "If you need to leave me behind, I want you to do it."

"I won't."

"Elly . . ."

"Adar, you're the only friend I have."

He studied her. "What about Sakari?"

Her gaze hardened with determination. "Sakari is trapped inside herself. I'm going to coax her out. Like Chriel coaxed me out."

"Elice, what's happened to her family—it's the Sundering."

"Isn't there even a chance this is caused by the Summer Queen?

"If that were true, the destruction wouldn't be just as bad in her realm. And it is."

Elice bit the inside of her check. "I can't, Adar. I can't believe that she—that I—could have caused this."

"You said that before. I don't understand."

She wrapped her arms around herself as if to hold herself together. "Whether because of the Sundering, as you say, or sabotage from the Summer Queen, what hope do we have?"

Adar cocked her a grin. "I can hope for you."

He could tell she didn't really believe him, but her gaze was soft and open. She trusted him, completely and without guile. Her mother had been right about that. Such innocence, like newly fallen snow graced with the golden light of morning. Again, he wanted to kiss her lips, to know if she tasted as fresh and clean as she always smelled. To see for himself if her mouth was as giving and open as the rest of her.

Yet he hesitated. He shouldn't be doing this. It wasn't fair to her. Then she closed her eyes and tipped her mouth up, and he didn't care about kingdoms and enemies, fire and ice. There was only her.

Just before his mouth would have met hers, there was a sound like a sudden gust of wind. They both started. "Stay here," Elice said softly. Had the fairies found them? Was that the sound of their rushing wings as they charged?

Adar tensed as she crawled a little farther through the hole and stuck her head out. But then she looked back at him and grinned. "Look!"

Chiding himself for a fool for trying to kiss her, he pulled himself up alongside her. Backlit by a passing iceberg was a pod of humpback whales below the surface of the sea. They churned in a circle, releasing rings of bubbles that turned the black water jade.

"What are they doing?"

Elice smiled knowingly. "Just listen." Adar could hear them then, their haunting wails, almost like music. "They're calling to each other," she said.

They watched as the circle tightened until the whales were swimming head to tail. Then they disappeared altogether, leaving the ring of jade. Adar opened his mouth to ask where they went, when they suddenly breeched. Totally exposed, three mouths gaped large enough to swallow a ship whole. Inside, he could see squirming masses of fish just before the jaws slipped closed, water pouring from the animals' baleens.

Adar and Elice lay on their bellies, watching the creatures perform the same technique over and over again until he started shivering even while holding her hand.

She rested her chin on her laced fingers. "We're like them you know—we work together, and all the facts stacked against us don't stand a chance."

Then something appeared on the horizon—rivers of green undulating across the sky. Adar's mouth came open in wonder, for it was beautiful and ethereal and primal.

But Elice drew in a quick breath. "My mother is looking for us." After sealing the hole so only a little air snaked through, Elice insisted that Adar retreat into the depths of the cavern.

Sick with worry, she stayed beside him, keeping hold of him to stay the cold while he slept. She looked up when Sakari slipped into the cavern, the other girl's movements made a little clumsy by her bulky clothing. Elice wondered what Sakari looked like under all those furs. Did her body match her round face, or was she lithe and graceful?

"How's Adar?" Sakari asked.

"Still sleeping." Elice pressed her lips together. He'd been sleeping almost constantly for two days, only waking long enough to eat the food she and Sakari had forced down him. Elice was grateful for the other girl's help.

Sakari crouched beside Adar and brushed back some curls from his forehead, then held her hand there. "His fever has broken," she said finally.

Elice let out a breath in relief. "Then he only needs to regain his strength and he'll be fine." She reclined against the wall of snow. "Has the current started to take us east yet?"

Sakari looked back in the direction of the corridor that led to their viewing shelf. "It's hard to tell. Everything appears the same from this far out to sea."

When she fled the palace, Elice had lost all the landmarks she normally used to gauge the time of day by the position of the sun. So, not only was she feeling lost, she was also disoriented, with no idea what time it was, or even whether it was day or night. It was enough to make her dizzy. "Did any of it look familiar to you?"

Sakari shrugged. "I was a small girl when last I passed through this village. But it can't be much farther."

"Did you come through with your family?"

Sakari's expression closed off.

"I know what it's like," Elice said softly.

"You couldn't possibly know." Sakari's voice was bitter.

Elice gave a long sigh. "When I was thirteen years old, my father died. All these years, my mother has blamed the Summer Queen, but it was really my fault. I spent the next six years trying to make it up to her, but . . ." Elice let her words trail off.

"How could a child be responsible for the death of a man?"

Elice studied Adar's face, the dark circles under his eyes, his thick, curling hair, which he always wore pulled back. Her father's hair had been even curlier, turning frizzy when he would pull his hands through it. As he had done that day. Elice tried to stop the memories before they went any further. But it was like trying to bottle up a blizzard.

"My queen," the wolf fairy Lowl had said in her growling voice, "this is a trap. It has to be. Nelay will never forgive the deaths of her par—"

Ilyenna had shot the wolf fairy a look that silenced her mid-word. "Leave us."

159

Slouched in one of the chairs in the library, thirteen-year old Elice had glared at the fairy. After all, it was Lowl who took her mother away at summer's end. And it was Lowl her father always called "warmonger" under his breath.

With a cool glance at Elice, the fairy dropped her long nose in submission and flew from the room. Elice's mother waved a hand, and a gentle wind slipped from her fingertips, shutting the doors after the fairy. Then the Winter Queen resumed staring out the windows, her eyes dark like the depths of the churning sea. Elice's father stepped away from his daughter and cupped his wife's face in his hands.

Ilyenna's eyes slipped closed. "I'm so tired, Rone. Tired of war. Tired of leaving you for six months every year to oversee the battles."

"Then seek for peace."

Ilyenna let out a long breath. "Nelay killed my brother—she killed Bratton."

Rone's thumbs stroked her cheeks. "No. The war killed Bratton."

"That hasn't stopped Nelay from blaming me for her parents' deaths."

Elice was so tired of this argument. It seemed her mother and father had it every year, but nothing ever changed.

"Remember what I told you that day so long ago? You still have the same soul, Ilyenna. The soul of a healer."

Whenever the Winter Queen got that unyielding, sharp look to her eyes, Elice's father would talk about Ilyenna's soul.

Rone ducked down, catching her gaze. "War cannot stop war, Ilyenna. Only peace can do that."

She sighed. "What if Lowl is right? If this is a trap and Nelay manages to kill me, you and Elice will be helpless."

He grunted. "Do you have so little faith in me?"

Elice's mother pursed her lips. "You'll be at the complete mercy of whomever the fairies choose as their new queen."

Elice held up her own hands, and a blizzard raged from one palm to the next. "I'm not exactly helpless, Mother."

Rone grinned at her. "Neither am I." Ilyenna didn't look convinced, and Rone gathered her into his arms. "It won't come to that. We have been at war with Nelay for over three decades. You said yourself the magic is starting to deteriorate. Nelay has to have sensed this as well."

Ilyenna let out a long breath. "I hope you're right."

Rone smiled and kissed her forehead. "You'll see. Everything is going to change after this."

Ilyenna seemed to melt under Rone's gentle gaze. "For you, I'll try." She made a sound low in her throat and they kissed—this time on the mouth.

Elice curled her upper lip in disgust, wondering if she would be able to keep her breakfast down. Her father turned to her with a twinkle in his eye and burst into laughter.

Ilyenna gazed down at Elice. "Promise to look after your father while I'm gone? Don't let anything happen to him."

"It's not like you care, Mother. You're never here anyway."

Ilyenna's gaze hardened. "I have a war to run."

"And that war is more important than your family." It was not a question.

"Elice," Rone warned.

She pushed herself up from the chair. "You run your war and your fairies. But let me go. Let me see the world."

Rone rested a calming hand on Ilyenna's shoulders. "We've talked about this. It isn't safe."

"Because of her," Elice spat. "If she made peace, I could have a future. But instead, I'm trapped in *her* past." She turned on her heel and stormed from the room.

Harpoon and knives in hand, she left her cave in time to see her mother's enormous purple-and-green wings fill the horizon and then slowly fade. But she left behind a smear of color in the sky to keep back the dark. Elice trekked along the shore. She knew she could survive on her own—she'd hunted by herself enough times. And though her mother refused to let her have a map, the queendom had to meet up with Svass eventually. Elice had decided then and there to start walking and not stop. To never go back.

She had followed the shore, the dark sky cut nearly in half by the huge glacier that rose up beside her. She walked for hours, until she was tired and hungry and her feet hurt. She should have brought something to eat. Something to sleep on. But she could make do with a bed of snow, and she could hunt along the way. She swam out into the ocean and worked a few mussels free. Back on shore, she pried them open with her knife and ate her fill.

Her back against the glacier, she watched the waves coming in. She heard footsteps and turned to see her father's dark silhouette against the light reflecting off the textured velvet of the waters.

"Elice, it's time to come home."

She pushed herself to her feet. "I'm never coming home."

Her father tipped his head to the side. "But you don't know where you're going . . . or what you're leaving behind."

"Like Mother leaves us behind?"

"I'm tired and I'm worried about her. Let's go." He turned, obviously assuming Elice would follow.

"I'm not going anywhere!" she screamed.

Her voice echoed off the rough face of the glacier—echoed all around them. There was a bone-rattling rumble.

"Elice!" her father cried. "Run!"

A crash tore through the night. The glacier face collapsed, rushing toward her. Elice gaped up at it, frozen with horror.

"Elice!" her father yelled as he ran for her. "Wrap yourself up in ice!"

A thousand times, she had obeyed her father as he'd trained her to fight. A thousand times she had trusted him. She did so again, wrapping herself up in ice as the avalanche of snow blocked out all light and sound.

Elice woke to a fairy hovering over her, calling to someone out of sight. At first, Elice couldn't connect the fairy with a name or how she knew her, but eventually Elice recognized Chriel and understood the words she was saying. The sky beyond the fairy was the inky black of midwinter, bands of a poison-green aurora shifting above her. "Send for the queen!" Chriel was shouting.

Elice was trapped in ice. She pulled it into herself and braced herself on one arm, trying to understand what had happened. There were dozens of snow fairies, all hovering, watching her with impassive gazes. Chriel darted in front of her, blocking her view. "Princess, I need you to come with me back to the palace. Now."

Elice rubbed at the ache pounding behind her forehead. "Where's my father?"

The fairy darted toward Elice and back again, as if trying to herd her. "To the palace, child. Now."

Elice started to push to her feet when she caught sight of her father's hand, sticking out of the snow. The rest of him was buried. Suddenly she realized what the fairies had been doing, and why they had stopped. Scrambling to his side, Elice sucked the snow into herself.

"No, Princess," Chriel pled, tugging on Elice's hair.

The snow stormed back inside Elice, revealing her father's face, blue and covered in a layer of frost. "I can save him!" she cried out. She took his hand in hers and drew the cold into herself. His body went limp, but his eyes didn't open. He was so still. And somehow, he didn't look like her father.

Elice knew healing—her mother had taught her all that she knew. She held her fingers under her father's nose, waiting for the reassuring puff of breath against her skin. But there was nothing. She pressed her ear to his chest, waiting for the thump of his heart to sound against her ear. There was only silence.

He was gone, and he would never come back. It was Elice's fault. If she hadn't run away—had thought to wrap him in a pod of ice instead of herself—he would have survived. She couldn't cry. The tears wouldn't come. So she had sat in the absolute silence of winter, not even a breeze playing across the mountain, and had waited for her mother to come.

Elice shuddered and shut the memory down. Twin tears plunged down her cheeks. Sakari's forehead rested on her drawn knees. Elice thought the other girl might be crying. "My mother believed Nelay lured her away so she could start the avalanche that killed my father," Elice said pensively. "She would never believe me when I told her it was me."

Sakari finally spoke. "You were a child. You didn't mean to hurt him."

"Doesn't matter what I meant, my father is still dead."

Sakari swallowed loudly. "That I understand. I tried so hard to give my brothers my share of the food." Her voice dropped to a whisper. "Why is it that they should die and I should live?"

Elice stared, her eyes unfocused. "I ask myself that same question every day."

They were quiet for a time, and then Sakari said, "Does it ever get any easier?"

"Yes," Elice answered softly. "But it never gets easy."

Together, they returned to the ice shelf and silently watched the ocean slip by. Their specially designed iceberg caught the current and wind, propelling them much faster than Elice had thought it could. Circular ice floes bumped into each other, the constant collision leaving a slightly raised buildup of slush on the edges—like the lily pads Elice had read about. A bird suddenly gave a startled cry, and Elice placed her hand over Sakari's arm to signal her to keep quiet. The other girl didn't question her as Elice silently filled in the opening before them, leaving only a small hole to look out of.

On wings of pure white, half a dozen fairies flitted past. Elice opened her mouth in a silent gasp. From experience, she knew those wings were softer than rabbit fur. These fairies were smaller than most, but that's where any illusion of a gentle creature ended. Their eyes were beady and black, their teeth rodent-like and sharp as needles. What Elice could see of their skin was pink with a short covering of fur. They were stoat fairies—relentless hunters with an excellent sense of smell and sight.

"It's stronger here," came a voice out of sight.

The fairies circled back into view, hovering. From this distance, they were indistinguishable from one another. It didn't much matter, though, for Elice hated them all. Most of the predatory fairies thought themselves superior, but the wolf fairies were a little playful, the bear fairies a bit sluggish and dense at times. But what the stoats lacked in size they made up for in cunning and viciousness.

"Let's circle it again," said another fairy.

Elice had thought that as long as she and her friends were out of sight, they'd be safe. She should have known better. She shut her eyes and closed tight all the iceberg's vents, including the one directly in front of Sakari and her.

"Still nothing," came a muffled voice.

"Perhaps it's the stink from the human village," said another.

"The scent is weaker when we fly that way. I say we find ice fairies to disintegrate this iceberg."

"The ice fairies are fluffy-headed, pretty fools."

"Yes, but they deal with snow and we do not."

The fairies' snarling was interrupted by a rending sound. Elice gasped silently and turned to Sakari, but the girl had buried her face in the snow and clamped her hands over her ears. Elice had no idea what was happening, but the sound went on long enough that it seemed it might never end.

Finally, the roaring subsided. Elice listened hard for the fairies but heard nothing. "What was that?" she whispered.

"Earth tremor," Sakari said, her voice muffled by the snow. "They come all the time now."

Cautiously, Elice pulled back a bit of the snow and glanced out. There were no fairies in sight. She and Sakari silently moved away from the hole. Once Elice was sure the creatures could no longer hear her, she rushed down to the main cavern.

Adar blinked up at her, his face shiny with sweat. "What was that?"

"We have to go. Now!" Elice said. She poured him a cup of blood to give him strength.

He didn't ask questions, just drank the blood without complaint as Sakari gathered up their few supplies. Elice pulled Adar to his feet and started out. She didn't bother going up the path she'd made before. Instead, she forged a new one straight through the heart of the iceberg. At the same time, she was filling all the other crevices and caverns with packed snow to hide that anyone had been there.

When they neared the outside she paused, dissipating the snow more slowly, watching and waiting. They were at sea level, and the ocean was still, almost glasslike. "I don't see them," Elice reported, "and I don't dare wait any longer."

"We're with you," Adar said from behind her.

Elice whipped out her cold and froze the frazil ice into place. Determined that nothing would hurt her friends, she made the ice deep and thick. She was surprised when a whole swath of ocean froze solid. Maybe Adar was right and her magic was stronger than she'd ever imagined. She stepped out cautiously onto it, the once-slushy edges of the frazil ice crunching beneath her boots. She checked for any signs of seals below, but could only see large white bubbles stacked on top of each other a dozen deep. Even if there were seals, they weren't getting through that.

"Come on," Elice said to the others.

"Smoke." Sakari pointed to a dirty-looking haze to the south. "The village must be that way."

For the better part of an hour, with heads down and hoods up, they hurried across the solid sheet of sea ice toward an inlet. At one point, they crossed onto naturally formed ice, the surface going from smooth to jumbled, and their pace slowed accordingly. Elice kept glancing back at Adar, but she could see little more than the vapor of his breath trailing past his furry hood, leaving a rim of hoar frost in its wake.

She didn't like being out in the open like this—they were exposed for miles in all directions. Forming icebergs to hide them would draw even more attention, so that idea was out. Finally, they were almost to the shore, close enough that Elice could make out the texture of the sheer fronts of the glaciers. Her connection to winter was open so wide that she started at the feeling of no longer being alone. It was almost like she was being watched.

Then Elice realized she always felt that shift in her magic when a large group of fairies came near, as if her magic allowed her to sense them. "They're coming back. Run!"

"I can't," Adar panted. One look at him confirmed it was true. His face was pale, his shoulders hitched against the cold.

"We have to hide," Sakari said stiffly.

Elice's attention turned to the sea ice beneath them. If it was thick enough, they might be able to hide inside it. She shifted some into herself, creating a pockmark big enough for them to fit inside on the surface. What she found beneath, however, wasn't seawater but empty darkness. She let out a trickle of aurora light and was shocked to see the bare sea floor glimmering wetly about a story below.

"The tide's gone out," Sakari said, relief in her voice. She hurried in front of them and dropped down without a moment's hesitation.

Elice and Adar shared looks of concern. But she could feel the fairies coming closer. "Hurry," she whispered. He sat down before falling forward, Elice a beat behind him.

She broke through a thin layer of ice to splash into a puddle on the rocky bottom. Here, it smelled strongly of fish. She promptly closed the hole above them and let the aurora trickle along the bottom of the buckled sea ice, revealing a maze of jagged edges, pockets of emptiness between the angular pieces. Everything gleamed with a thin layer of ice. Spines of hoar frost as long as her fingers glittered wickedly in the light.

Elice hurried after Sakari, every step breaking off spines and plowing through ice-covered puddles. They turned sideways to slip past a mound of sharp-edged mussels growing on the side of a large rock. The sharp edges cut her hands.

"What do we do when the tide comes?" Adar asked skeptically.

Sakari didn't look back. "Sometimes we come under the ice at low tide for mussels. Everyone knows the stories of those who didn't make it out."

"Not exactly reassuring," Adar muttered.

Sakari came up to a huge wall of ice blocking their way and turned left. "Which is why we must hurry."

"How much time do we have before the tide comes back in?" Adar asked.

Sakari huffed. "I don't know how long it's been out, but half an hour at most."

Elice slipped on a chunk of slimy seaweed. Adar caught her arm and steadied her, wincing as her weight pulled on his bad shoulder. "I don't know if this is a good idea."

Elice studied Sakari's retreating form. "The smell of the fish should cover our scent. We just have to be out of the fairies' line of sight by the time the tide comes back."

They hurried along the eerie cavern. Crabs scuttled out of sight, claws clacking. Starfish gleamed. An octopus in a deep crevice dragged itself limply out of view, its eyes reflecting weirdly as it watched them.

The water level rose until the travelers were splashing through water up to their ankles. Elice kept her hand firmly in Adar's to protect him from the cold. Sakari splashed to a halt before a chunk of sea ice that blocked off their progression. She pushed away a piece of frosty seaweed that dangled from the ice. She started left, then turned back to the right before rounding on Elice and Adar.

"We'll have to backtrack." Fear tinged Sakari's voice.

Elice felt the seawater coming up her ankles. "We don't have time." She forged ahead, pulling the ice and snow back into winter and creating a tunnel through the blockage. Finally, they reached what had to be the shore, with the ground inclining sharply.

As the water came back, the ice shifted, the chaotic buckles of sea ice leveling out. Even when Elice crouched down, the ice brushed her back. Water dripped beneath her collar and inched up her legs, until she had no choice but to let go of Adar and crawl through rocks and seaweed, the heavy ice weighing oppressively over her.

"Elice," he said breathlessly. He didn't have to say anything else—she could hear the strain in his voice. Her legs and arms were soaked, the front of her torso damp. She couldn't imagine how bitterly cold this must feel after his fever. With no way to make a fire to warm him, he was already in grave danger.

Fairies or no, it was time to surface.

Elice formed an opening above them and hauled herself up. She peeked over the ice and found her glacier that was now a speck in the distance. It was too far away for her to detect any fairies. "Let's hope they gave up when they found the glacier empty and our scent trail gone."

She climbed out and reached back to help Sakari and Adar, who was shivering hard. Sakari eased him to the ground. "Help me take his clothes off."

"Easy now, ladies," he said through chattering teeth. "There's enough of me for both of you."

At his teasing, Elice bit her lip in worry. He was frightened. Careful to keep a hand on him to protect him from the cold, she helped Sakari pull off his boots and pants. Sakari briskly rubbed the fur through the snow.

"What are you doing?" Elice asked as she turned the water in Adar's boots to snow and shook it out.

"Caribou fur is better than seal. The snow soaks up the water." Sakari started dressing him, Elice helping her.

Adar looked at Sakari in disbelief. "They're dry."

She was already pulling off her own clothes.

"I could do that for you," Elice offered.

Thanking her, Sakari handed over her boots, and Elice shook out the resulting snow. Not wanting to be wet, she did the same for herself, with Adar's hand on her neck so she could draw away the cold. Once they finished, they helped Adar to his feet, each woman positioning herself under his arm, and headed toward the smoke. The village was partially obscured by a rise.

Elice cleared a path through the snow, and they crossed the side of the inlet on bare ground. On the other side was a cluster of tents built in a protected spot between three hills a safe distance from the ocean. Elice's freeze hadn't touched the water here, so it was black and open, spotted with ice floes and icebergs.

Soon she could see the tents were made of sealskins stretched across bleached whale bones. The people on the shore didn't seem to notice the three strangers approaching them; they were too busy looking out over the ocean to the east. Elice followed their gazes and made out people in small boats barely big enough for a single person. They were trailing behind a bowhead whale, close enough that it could swamp all their boats with a powerful flick of its tail.

The lead man thrust his paddle toward the whale, and when he drew it back, blood dripped off a blade attached to the end. A pool of blood circled the animal—the hunters must have already wounded it.

Elice would have never guessed something as small as those little boats would have the ability to kill a massive whale, but the animal didn't even seem alarmed. A commotion drew her gaze back to the village—they'd obviously been spotted. By the time they reached the village, a group of eight women were the only people to be seen, the children having vanished. The woman in the center was older, her dark face heavily lined. Her hair was nearly white, with a few gray strands here and there. The women behind, of varying ages, had Sakari's almond-shaped eyes and dark features. Elice couldn't help but stare. She'd never before seen so many people at once.

Sakari stepped forward. "I am Sakari. My uncles are Anuni-aq and Kiviuq from the northeast. We have traded with your people for caribou hides."

The oldest woman nodded. "I am Tapeesa. I know your family, Sakari, but I do not know this woman." Her gaze turned to Elice.

"It was her," whispered a woman partially concealed behind Tapeesa. "She's the one who made the path through the ice and snow. It went into her and disappeared." When the young woman caught Elice looking at her, she started and took another step behind Tapeesa, whose gaze narrowed at Elice.

"Are you the Winter Queen, who controls winter as if it were a toy to be played with?"

Adar sighed and said in Clannish, "Elly, we have to work on your discretion."

"She's the Winter Queen's daughter, Elice," Sakari clari-fied.

The old woman lifted her chin. "The Winter Queendom is much like her queen—harsh and merciless. Yet we survive. Thrive even. Until the last few years. Tell me, daughter of winter, why we have lost favor with the queen?"

"Please, my friend is sick," Elice said. "He needs a warm fire. A place to rest."

"After all the damage your queen has caused?" Tapeesa asked.

"Then send us away with a couple of sleds and the dogs to pull them," Sakari said.

The woman glowered. "You would take our livelihoods from us?"

"We would give them back," Elice said quickly.

"We only need to borrow them long enough to get out of the queendom," Adar said.

"And how would you return them to us?" Tapeesa wanted to know.

One of the younger women spoke up. "We cannot send them away hungry and sick. It is not our way."

Tapeesa clenched her teeth. "Fine, Maliq, find them a tent and some supplies. You can help them set it up somewhere far from our village."

"That is not the way of the Svass," Sakari retorted. The two women traded glares.

Tapeesa turned on her heel to stride back to the village, calling out orders in rapid succession. Elice and Adar shared a hopeless look. Without those dogs, they had no hope of reaching the border before the last day of Winter's End—now only three days away.

"Adar . . ." She let her voice trail off, not knowing how to give voice to her hopelessness.

"We need those dogs," he ground out. "We'll steal them if we have to."

Elice cast a nervous look back at the men on the kayaks. Ropes trailed from around their middles to the whale, which had gone still.

Sakari followed her glance. "The men would hunt you down for trying," she said in a low voice.

Adar opened his mouth to argue when the ground suddenly bucked. Elice's hands flew out to catch herself and she stared at the pitching ground, half expecting a giant fissure to open up beneath her feet.

17

In the village, one of the tents collapsed. Back the way Elice and the others had come, a small avalanche plowed through the fissure she'd created in the snow before spilling harmlessly into the ocean. After a long while, the shaking subsided. Elice instinctively turned toward Adar, whose worried gaze was already raking over her. She nodded to let him know she was all right, and his expression relaxed a fraction.

"Sakari?" Elice called out.

"Another one," Sakari said from the other side of Adar, her hands fisted at her sides.

They helped each other to their feet. Tapeesa was already up and storming toward them. Sakari took up a defensive stance in front of Adar and Elice.

"This is the Winter Queen's work!" barked Tapeesa. "Her bloodthirsty tirades have already killed dozens of—"

The woman's outburst was interrupted by a piercing scream. Elice's gaze snapped to the villagers, who were either running or gazing slack-jawed out over the ocean. She spun around and followed their gazes. The surf was rapidly disappearing, the sea drawing back to leave gaping fish and limp sea plants.

"What is that?" came Adar's voice beside her.

Tapeesa cried out in grief, calling for her sons in their boats. Other women screamed for their children, commanding them to flee up the mountains. Children emerged from their hiding places behind the village. Some heeded their mothers and began to scamper up the rise. Others burst into wails. One little girl covered her face with her hands. A woman swooped down and snatched her from the ground, then ran on. Elice saw another child peeking out from the hood of the woman's parka.

Elice looked back at the hunters. A giant swell sucked them back. They pulled on their paddles with frantic sweeps, but the sea kept hauling them up and up and up, until a wave as tall as a mountain formed.

Holding to Elice's arm, Adar dragged her away from the shore. Sakari was already running, her hood slipping off as she bent down to snatch a screaming toddler and sprint after the others. Tapeesa, her face determined, was cutting the lines that tethered the dogs. Elice knew the woman didn't expect to survive.

Elice glanced back as the wave blocked out the sun, casting a dark shadow across the village. She jerked her arm out of Adar's hold. "No." She said it as much to him as she did the wave threatening to destroy these people.

"Elice!" he called after her.

I'm stronger than I know, she thought as she planted both her feet. The wave tipped ominously over the hunters. She closed her eyes and opened herself to the winter—the cold, the ice, the frost, the surging blizzard and merciless wind. She pulled all of it in until there was nothing left to take. She opened her eyes to find a ball of silver-white light dancing in her hand, so bright it was nearly impossible to look at. Just like the one her mother had used to kill Chriel.

Elice didn't have time for shock—she simply threw the ball at the water. It slammed into the ocean in a brilliant flash of light. With a massive crack, the ocean and its monster wave froze solid. Light shimmered and arched, thousands of droplets of frozen water falling with a tinkling sound. A little farther down, a particularly large iceberg perched precariously at the tip of the wave broke free and pitched forward. It crashed, ice and snow scattering across the tops of the frozen waves.

She had a moment of panic. What if she'd just frozen the hunters solid? But then one of them cried out, tumbled from his kayak, and sat up, gaping at the frozen wave above them. Elice let out her breath in a rush.

"Fire and burning," Adar said from beside her.

The hunters tested the ice with their paddles, then carefully stepped out of their kayaks. Elice eased onto the naked sea floor and nearly fell. Adar, who was right behind her, steadied her, and then nearly toppled himself. The ice was slick. Elice didn't usually make slippery ice.

She tried to draw on winter again to add some textured snow, but there was nothing to take, for the magic was completely depleted. Did her mother experience the same thing when she did this, or was it because Elice was weaker? Had her mother felt as helpless and insignificant as Elice now did?

Elice, Adar, and Sakari left the shore and moved, slipping and sliding, across the ice, passing hundreds of frozen sea stars, sea spiders, and even a rigid seal. But as Elice and Adar approached the men, they held out their oars, which were tipped with wicked-looking spears. Elice took a startled step back. She didn't have any magic left to fight them.

Adar moved protectively in front of her. "She just saved your lives," he said in Svass.

The men slowly lowered the spears. One of them, who looked to be in his mid-thirties, motioned toward her with his chin. "Are you the queen?"

"Her daughter," Adar answered him. "And who are you?"

"Aklaq," the man said evenly. "Do you mean us any harm, winter's daughter?"

Elice shook her head. "My name is Elice. We came for your help."

Aklaq's spear oar fell to his side. "What could one as powerful as you need from us?"

"Your dogs," Adar said. "But Tapeesa has already refused us."

The man rubbed some frost off his chin. "My mother might reconsider now."

He turned back to his fleet of stranded kayaks, partially frozen in the ice. The dead whale's tail protruded from the wave, frozen solid. Elice noticed movement beyond, and her mouth came open as a pod of whales approached the floating carcass—so she hadn't frozen the entire ocean solid, just a very thick layer of it.

The way the wave had frozen, the pod was at eye level. She watched as they swam around, nudging the limp body with their noses. They called to one another in a mournful song—Elice could feel the vibrations of it through her feet. One of them paused, and she could have sworn it looked right at her. It was large enough it probably could have crushed the ice, drowning them all.

She stepped forward, rested her bare hand on the ice, and tried to communicate that she was sorry. Whether or not the creature understood, it turned and slowly swam away, the rest of the whales following it.

"That's why I save the ones I can," Elice said to Adar. "I hate that they have to die so we can live."

Coming up beside her, he pulled off his mitten with his teeth. Then he took hold of her hand without a word. She was distracted from the faint outline of the departing whales by the sound of chipping ice. She turned to find the men trying to dig out their kayaks.

She opened herself to winter and found some dregs of magic had returned, so she used it to encase the kayaks and the carcass in snow. The whale immediately came free, skidding down the ice and coming to rest on the seabed with the rest of the dead and dying creatures.

And then Elice's magic was gone again.

The men shot her quite a few nervous glances as they pulled their kayaks free and lifted them onto their shoulders. Slipping and sliding, the group trekked down from the ocean to the carcass resting on the seafloor.

"Aklaq, ask her how long it will hold," said one of the men.

Aklaq turned to Elice, but before he could repeat the question she said, "I'm not sure. I've never done this before."

"Start butchering," Aklaq called. "We won't waste the meat." The men took out long knives and began cutting into the whale's rubbery skin. Adar stepped forward and touched the animal's body. "It feels like a boiled egg."

Aklaq handed him a piece of the skin. "Eat, it will keep you warm."

Adar started chewing . . . and kept on chewing. Elice knew from experience that it would take him a while. "We have three days left to reach the border between the lands of winter and summer," she told Aklaq. "And we have to move fast. Will you help us?"

He paused to gaze up at her. There was blood on his hands. "I will help you. We will take my dogs." He turned to the others, his eyes asking a silent question. Elice didn't dare look. What if no one else agreed to help them?

"Tikaani will come as well," Aklaq said when he turned back to her.

That's two more than I thought we'd have, Elice mused.

"We must see our people to safety," Aklaq went on. "Elice, if you would tell the women to pack the tents up the mountain and bring us the dogs. We cannot be here when the ice melts."

She turned to Adar, who was still chewing. "When we get a tent set up on that ridge, I want you to rest in it."

He grunted. "I keep telling you, I'm hard to kill."

She narrowed her gaze on him. His chewing slowed and he finally swallowed. "You can be scary, you know that, right?" he teased. She gave him a toothy grin. He shivered. "Someone should light a fire—the smoke will keep the fairies at bay. I volunteer to tend said fire."

Aklaq's eyes narrowed in thought. "We have some moss left. Makes lots of smoke."

Elice didn't leave Adar's side until he was in a newly erected tent at the top of the hill, a cheery fire burning beside him. He had barely lain down before he was fast asleep. While he slept, Elice and Sakari helped the women pack up tents and supplies. In a few hours, the whole camp had been moved to the top of the mountain. The dog sleds hauled the last few loads of whale meat up the tallest hill, where it was cut up into smaller pieces and laid out to dry in the arid winter air. The whole village worked together, eating as they went.

Elice volunteered to help with the butchering, but Tapeesa politely refused the offer. Sakari shot Elice an apologetic look and made to follow Tapeesa. Elice grasped her arm. "Thank you, Sakari. If not for you, I don't know if Adar and I would have made it this far."

Sakari gave her a half grin. "He's heavier than he looks."

Elice chuckled. "Believe me, I know." She sobered. "But it's not just that. You stood up for us."

Sakari stared at the ground. "It's hard to care about people when you're always afraid you might lose them. But I think not caring is worse."

She knelt beside the other women and went to work. Elice watched her work and wondered, *Will there ever be a place where I belong like that?*

Elice turned away. She had other things to worry about— like reaching the border before Winter's End. She wandered to the next hill, where the dogs were gorging themselves on whale blubber. They were relatively small animals, at least compared to the only other land animals she knew—polar bears.

She bent down by one and observed the way it tore away chunks of meat, then swallowed without really chewing. The dogs' faces and mannerisms reminded her of a leopard seal, only, of course, the dogs were smaller and more muscularly built and had legs instead of flippers. "You can pet them," said a voice from behind her.

Still crouched, Elice pivoted to find Tikaani behind her. He was a young man, not much older than her. He carried more meat to the dogs, which barked and strained at their tethers. Elice reached out and stroked the back of the nearest dog. The fur wasn't nearly as soft and sleek as seal fur. The dog seemed to like the attention, though, for he crowded her and licked her cheek with a smelly tongue. She laughed a little, suddenly wishing she'd had one of her own in the palace.

"I've heard stories of a palace taller than a mountain and grander than anything we can imagine," Tikaani said without looking at her. "Though your clothes are worn, I can tell they were once fine. You don't even need to wear a parka. Why would you defy your mother by leaving?"

Shame knifed through Elice. She reached for her magic out of habit and found it weak but serviceable. Wanting to test herself further, she called forth a mild blizzard with swirling currents of air. She found that if she bent the currents and wanted them to stay, they did. So she bent and twisted and turned until a face peered back at her—the face of her mother.

Elice released the magic, and the face scattered across her lap.

Tikaani crouched beside her. "I do not wish to be cruel, but I need more than just gratitude if you wish me to risk my life and, by extension, the lives of my family."

She forced herself to face him. He had the typical Svass dark skin, round face, and narrow eyes, and there was determination in his expression. He was handsome, too, with dimples in both cheeks and a bright smile—she'd seen it when he'd greeted the dogs.

"Because I want to be free," Elice finally said. "I want a people, like you have a people."

"None of us are truly free. We are all at the mercy of life." Tikaani tipped his head to the side as he studied her. "What of the other two you travel with?"

She let out a long breath. "I don't think my mother will hurt Sakari—she has no reason to. But Adar . . . she nearly drowned him and then set a pack of seals and then polar bears on us. All after she promised she wouldn't hurt him." Elice shook her head. "I don't trust her to let him go even if I did go back to her."

Tikaani slowly nodded. "So it's love then, and not fear, that drives you."

Elice opened her mouth to argue with him. She certainly wasn't in love with Adar. He was irritating and inconsiderate and loud. But the words wouldn't come. Before she could formulate a response, Tikaani had walked away.

18

L ater that day, Elice settled into the first dog sled, with Aklaq on the runners behind her. Sakari followed behind with Adar. Tikaani came last, his sled holding a large load of whale meat and blubber. Aklaq had informed Elice that it was more for the dogs than for themselves. Before her, the sixteen dogs yipped and danced at their harnesses. One let out a long howl that sent a shudder through Elice.

"My bones protest this," Tapeesa said sourly.

"That's because you are old, Mother," Aklaq said without looking at her.

Tapeesa huffed. "We need you and Tikaani here to protect the people."

A great cracking sound whipped through the group, making the dogs jump and yip. Elice twisted around and watched as a fissure split the center of the frozen wave. Everyone seemed to hold a collective breath as fractures spread faster and farther. Water shot out in places, the holes that let them through widening and breaking apart until the sea was released with a roar. It surged forward. Elice opened herself to winter. Though she still wasn't at full power, she might be able to put a barrier between the people and the surging wave.

182

The water slammed into the protected cove where the village had been and surged up the mountain, but instead of continuing toward the village's new site, it spread between the hills until it reached the glacier. It pooled and rose, eating away the landscape one churning wave at a time. Elice prepared herself, but the water halted, milling about the mountains and going no higher.

Aklaq turned back to her, anger in his eyes. "And what protection could I offer against that wave, Mother? It would have killed us all."

His mother's eyes gleamed with unshed tears. "When gods and mankind mix, mankind always loses. You are meddling in the affairs of immortals. Such a union will not bode well for us who have no power in the world of fairies."

Aklaq fixed his gaze ahead of them. "Elice saved my life. She saved your life. She saved the lives of my wife and my children. Now she asks for our help. I cannot deny her."

His mother scowled. "And what would you have us do while you're away?"

Aklaq sighed. "It's not much earlier than we normally leave to hunt caribou. Tikaani and I will go ahead and start the hunt. The rest of you follow along after you finish drying the whale meat."

Tapeesa took a step closer. Elice couldn't help but notice the genuine fear in her eyes. Aklaq softened and leaned forward to press his forehead to hers. When she stepped back, a younger woman and five children took her place. Elice glanced back in time to see Tikaani press his forehead to a woman and three children who must have been his mother and siblings.

Elice shifted her gaze to Aklaq. "Am I wrong to ask this of you?"

He looked up from tying down some straps, his eyes determined. "Perhaps the queen shall kill me. I cannot know. But I can at least be as brave as the girl who owed me nothing and yet risked everything." Before Elice could protest, he called out to his dogs while releasing a lever on the side of the sled. The sled glided forward and picked up speed until the wind bit into Elice's cheeks and tugged tears from her eyes.

The landscape changed little as they crossed the hard-packed snow, always heading south. The dogs trotted on and on, seeming tireless and only pausing to eat snow and some meat before they were off again. The group broke for a late dinner, eating the same meat as the dogs.

Elice wandered among the group, drawing away the cold, though it was hardly necessary. She tended to Adar as well. His shoulder was out of the sling, and he could lift his arm above his head. The bite marks were scabbing over, the redness and swelling gone. He seemed stronger, too, and he kept everyone laughing with his jokes.

As they continued on, there were no animals, since there was nothing to support any creature so far inland. They stopped that night, and Elice formed a hollow mound of snow that looked like a large drift. The dogs packed into it, along with the people. With Adar on one side of her, and Sakari on the other, Elice slept hard and dreamless. The next day was much the same, but the landscape began to change. The weather became warm and the snow turned to slush, something Elice had rarely seen on land before.

She could make out a dark smudge in the distance. When she asked Aklaq about it, he said it was mountains—their destination. Elice settled back, watching as the mountains grew larger and began to take shape as sharp peaks covered in glaciers. She was so distracted she didn't notice anything amiss, even when the dogs began to cast nervous glances at the mountains taking shape around them.

It wasn't until Adar's voice cut through the slicing of the runners that Elice realized something was dreadfully wrong. "Cover your face!"

Not asking why, she pulled her fur muffler over her mouth and nose and ducked under her hood. She saw their dark shadow on the snow. Then she heard voices and knew it didn't matter whether she hid her face or not.

Of all the animals she'd nursed back to health, many had later died. But only one death had made her weep with rage. She'd come back to the cage to find nothing left of the icebird but feathers and blood. And though no fairies had ever entered Elice's smoky, underground cave before, she had instantly known which fairy had done it, for she could smell the stench of sulfur and rot. Wolverine fairies. Tenacious, cruel, and cunning. Even the bear fairies feared them. Only the wolf fairies stood against them, and then only because they banded together in an unbreakable pack.

Elice ripped back her hood and saw a pack of wolverine fairies circling Adar, the weak sunlight shining off their oily fur wings. She launched herself from the moving dog sled, anger and protectiveness rising within her alongside the cold. But the fairies did not attack—according to the bargain, they couldn't. Instead, one of them shot a greasy smile at Elice, fangs bared, and the whole flock turned, their wings beating as they flew away, no doubt heading to alert the Winter Queen of her daughter's whereabouts.

Elice launched out with her ice. A huge chunk wrapped around the center mass of fairies, dropping a dozen like stones. Five escaped, scattering in all directions. Running to keep them in sight, Elice shot ice after them, encasing one fairy after another, until she had all but one. It zagged back and forth, evading every shot of ice she sent its way. She felt someone approaching her from behind. Out of the corner of her eye, she saw Tikaani raise a bow.

"No!" she and Adar shouted at the same time.

But it was too late. The arrow flew true, dropping the fairy from the sky. Elice ran toward it, hardening the snow as she went so she didn't sink. When she found the creature, the arrow had nearly cut it in half. The fairy's blue blood spattered the fresh snow around it. Panting, the fairy shot her a vicious smile. And then it died. Elice staggered back.

"I don't understand," Tikaani said. "I stopped it. Isn't that what you wanted?"

Sakari ran up, standing shoulder to shoulder beside Elice. "It's them, isn't it? The fairies," Sakari whispered as if afraid the dying one might overhear her.

"It's a wolverine," Aklaq said as he peered down at the fairy. "But there was nothing there before!"

"It was a bird," Tikaani answered defensively. "And then it turned into a wolverine."

"It's a fairy," Adar said.

Elice bent down and scooped up one of the fairies frozen in a chunk of ice. It glared at her, and she could feel the growl through her fingers. "Without the Sight, all you can see is the lie. It must be a bit different for all of you." Elice closed her eyes, connected with the ice she'd just encased the fairies with, and made it self-sustaining. It would trap the creatures and take them out of the game until her mother dissipated the ice.

In disgust, Elice tossed away the ice-incased fairy. "Once they're dead, they can inhabit the bodies of their nearest creature. The one you shot and killed is already a fairy again. And she's flying to my mother."

Tikaani pursed his lips. "I'm sorry."

Elice shook her head. "You didn't know."

Sakari gazed at the young man. "I have never seen such marksmanship."

His stooped shoulders lifted a little and he blushed, seeming unable to look at her.

Oblivious, Adar was already headed back to the sled. "We have to hurry."

"The dogs can move faster if they don't have to pull us," Aklaq said.

"Isn't that the point of the dogs in the first place?" Adar asked.

"We run to rest the dogs," Aklaq explained. "If it gets really steep, we'll help push the sleds. When we're tired or the snow is deep and soft, the dogs will take over."

Elice made the snow hard and fast, and the people ran behind the dogs. It wasn't long before they were winding through a canyon that cut through the heart of the mountains.

"The tundra where the caribou grazed is on the other side," Aklaq informed her. She glanced back and met Adar's gaze.

He nodded to indicate he'd heard. "Can we make that in two days?"

Aklaq squinted into the distance. "We can try."

Elice turned so her companions wouldn't see the tension on her face. Ilyenna knew where they were. She would attack them, and soon.

Despite the urgency of the journey, or perhaps because of it, Aklaq insisted they stop to feed the dogs every few hours. He checked the animals' feet and rewrapped their paws in strips of supple leather. The dogs trotted on and on.

Taking a break meant resting in the sleds, and Elice and Adar had to rest more often than did the highmen. By the end of the day, their legs shook with exhaustion. Elice thawed some meat, and as she began passing out the allotments, she noticed Tikaani watching Sakari. Tikaani quickly glanced away whenever Sakari looked in his direction. And despite everything, despite all the fear and heartache and exhaustion, Elice smiled a secret smile.

She sat down beside Sakari and leaned in close. "Tikaani has been watching you."

The girl cast a discreet glance his way. "Did you see the way he shot that arrow? And of all the men in the village, he was the only one besides Aklaq to volunteer."

"You should go talk to him," Elice whispered.

Sakari started to shake her head but then must have changed her mind, because she straightened up, walked over to Tikaani, and sat beside him. She said something to him, and he gave her a shy smile.

Adar dropped down beside Elice and eyed her. "You've done something."

She blinked at him. "What?"

"Definitely." He nodded slowly. "You've got this look. Like you've slipped a beetle in the soup and no one's noticed though half the pot is gone."

Elice raised an eyebrow. "Do tribesmen eat beetles on purpose?"

"Not unless we have to. Or your older brother hides one in the stew."

She couldn't help but chuckle. "And you say raw meat is bad."

"Hey! I didn't actually eat the beetle," Adar exclaimed. "Laleh did. Which is unfortunate because she was the baby, so she didn't even know enough to squeal."

Elice narrowed her gaze on him. "How did any of them trust you?"

Adar grinned. "They didn't."

She rolled her eyes. Then she made them another shelter and they all crowded around inside. Despite her fear, she immediately fell into an exhausted sleep. She didn't even know until the next day that the highmen had kept watch in turns.

"This is our life," Aklaq said when she muttered something about how she should have helped. "It is not so hard for us. Take your rest, daughter of winter."

That morning, the group entered the mountain pass. A large river surged past them, silent under a thick layer of ice. As they climbed they passed ice-covered streams that flowed down from side canyons, feeding an ever-dwindling river. By mid-afternoon, they passed the summit, and the river disappeared altogether. It wasn't long before more streams created a new river that traveled in the opposite direction of the first. It increased in size and speed the farther they went.

Wary, Elice watched the sky. Her mother had to know where they were now, but she hadn't made a move to attack. No move to stop them even as the mountains grew in size, becoming mammoths that crowded in like an ever-tightening noose and forced the travelers onto the only path available to them—the river. So, they sliced across the snow-covered ice. Elice texturized the path as she ran beside the sled. The air sawed in and out of her lungs, and her body felt hot and disconnected, her lips tingling and numb. But unlike the last time she had faced off with her mother, Elice now knew she was at least as strong. She would hold her own, and she would keep her friends safe.

It was this awakening of power that allowed Elice to sense two things. First, the divide between winter and summer was close, and growing closer by the hour. She suspected that sometime the next day, they would cross it to safety. Second, she sensed how deep and swift the river churned below them. The two observations made her heart pound, for if her mother was to attack, it would be soon.

Therefore, when the lead dog's hackles rose and it looked off to the right, Elice did too. The other dogs started to notice something, too, and one of them let out a low growl. "Something's wrong," Elice murmured to Aklaq.

He leaned forward and spoke low. "We'll go faster if you get in the sled."

She did as she was told, her eyes scanning the craggy surface of the mountain. Aklaq climbed on the back of the sled and called to his dogs. The animals strained against their harnesses, their tongues hanging out. They rushed up between the steep mountains. From the corner of her eye, Elice saw a movement through the boulders. She whipped around and thought she saw a streak of white, but it was gone before she could be sure.

"Can I kill them this time?" Aklaq asked.

Elice wasn't sure what "them" was, but at this point it didn't matter much. "Yes."

He stepped onto the runners, drew his bow from its place beside her, and nocked three arrows. Elice strained to listen, to see, but she couldn't hear anything over the *whoosh* of the runners.

Another streak, this time to her right. Her head whipped around, but whatever it had been was gone again. "What is it?" she whispered.

"Wolves," Aklaq answered.

Elice's heart began to pound. And she knew. Her mother had sent Lowl after her. Of course she had. The wolf fairy was her most cunning general. Elice opened herself to winter, glancing back to see Tikaani with his bow at the ready. Adar gripped the ice knife she'd given him. Sakari held a bone knife, her gaze fierce and eager.

And then something launched itself at Elice, teeth snapping around her overtunic. Even as she felt the fabric rip, she locked eyes with the fairy riding on the wolf's back—Lowl. Elice sent a shock of cold into the animal, stopping its heart instantly. The wolf fairy only grinned viciously at her and flew backward. Fur exploded from the fairy's body, and she grew in size until she was an enormous white wolf. She howled, long and loud.

Over a dozen wolves leapt from behind boulders, launching themselves at the dogs. Wolves and dogs collided in a snarling mass, biting and tearing at each other's necks and flanks. Six wolves had attacked Aklaq's dogs. Elice wanted to shoot her cold at the animals, but she couldn't risk hitting the dogs. Aklaq launched himself in the midst of them, stabbing at the white fur of the wolves. Elice scrambled after him. She felt a moment of sorrow—these animals were being driven by the fairies, their will stripped away by their masters. And she was going to kill them for it.

She waited for an opening, then lunged to touch the animal's flank, stopping its heart with cold. Aklaq had already stabbed one wolf, sending bright blood bursting from the animal's white coat. Elice reached to touch another wolf just as the snarling animals turned. She felt an intense pressure in her hand and wasn't sure which of the animals had clamped down on her, but just as quickly it released her.

She staggered forward and touched another wolf, killing it instantly. With four wolves now dead, the dogs had vastly superior numbers. The remaining two wolves darted back into the mountains, leaving a trail of blood on the bright-white snow. Aklaq dropped to the side of one of his dogs. The animal's chest rose and fell as it panted. All the dogs were bleeding. One had an ear torn off.

Elice whipped around to check on the others. Adar and Sakari fended off their wolves and turned to help Tikaani. Elice took a step toward them, but then she saw them—a thousand ice fairies, their hands spread on the ice. Her gaze snapped to Lowl, who gave her a wolfish grin.

"Get off the ice!" Elice choked. "It was a diversion!" She felt Aklaq's eyes on her, but she couldn't look at him. Not when she could already feel the ice shattering under her feet. She channeled her power, driving it into the river, keeping it solid while the fairies worked against her—while her mother worked against her.

Adar hollered at the others and called to the dogs. Elice felt one of the sleds brush against her leg as it limped past. Beneath her, the ice cracked and splintered. She froze it back together. The fairies broke it apart. She froze it again. They broke it apart.

Elice was stronger than any one of them, but not all of them. She gave up trying to hold together anything but a bridge of ice leading to the riverbank. The rest of the ice fell away, revealing swift black water. Ahead of her, the men were coaxing the dogs, many of which were frozen in fear. Elice walked in a trail of their blood, ice falling away behind each of her steps.

The ice fairies converged, hundreds of them, all descending like a blizzard, for surely that's all the highmen could see. The bridge was shrinking, thinning, and Elice wondered if her mother would let her die. If she was trying to kill her. "Hurry," Elice gasped, sweat breaking out across her brow.

Aklaq was the first one onto the bank. Adar and Sakari were right behind him. Trailing in last was Tikaani. He was struggling with his dogs, which were balking and whining.

"I can't hold it," Elice cried.

Aklaq called out to him, "Leave the sled."

Tikaani cut the tethers. Elice trembled as the ice shattered and reformed, shattered and reformed. Each time, Tikaani lost his balance, making his progress slower. And then all the thousand little cracks stopped and one speared through the ice, severing Tikaani and Elice from the bank. She drew hard on winter, trying to fill the gap, but she was too late. The floe broke free, wobbling precariously and picking up speed. She started to increase its size, but it slammed into a boulder sticking out of the river and nosedived.

Elice's feet flew out from under her. Her hands whipped out and held onto the edge of the floe. For a split second Tikaani, still gripping his dogs, met her gaze, a calm knowing in his eyes. Then he skidded off the tipping ice and disappeared into the black water.

Elice stared in disbelief. From the shore, she was aware of shouting, but it seemed far away and unreachable. The ice floe dropped, water spilling over the side and drenching her, before twirling in a sickening circle.

She pulled herself to the edge and peered down, searching for any sign of Tikaani and preparing to form another ice floe under him the moment he surfaced. But the dark water revealed nothing of the terrified dogs or very brave young man. Elice thought of his mother and siblings, who had seen him off, and a chasm seemed to open up inside her. She ripped off her outer tunic and boots, formed a bubble around her head, and dove. She kicked downstream, searching the churning waters for Tikaani. She passed beneath the shadow of a layer of ice, the water turning even darker. Though she tried to control her respirations, they came fast. Elice was running out of air.

Remembering her newfound power, she lit up an aurora around her just in time to see herself rushing toward a huge boulder. She gathered her legs, trying to roll out of its path, but she broadsided it. All the air left her body in a *whoosh*. The ice bubble around her head shattered. She spun in a chaotic whirl of bubbles and water.

Her lungs ached, her body ached. Another moment and she would die. Elice did the only thing she could, surrounding herself with ice that floated into the shelf above her. She turned the ice above herself to snow and pushed herself out of the river that had become Tikaani's grave. The moment she felt the kiss of the wind, she collapsed, gasping and sobbing as the water soaking her clothes froze to the icy layer of snow.

She heard steps pounding toward her, felt the spray of snow as the person knelt beside her. Adar gathered her into his arms as the ice broke painfully around her. "I thought I'd lost you. I thought you were gone."

"Tikaani," she wailed.

Adar squeezed her hard, so hard it hurt. "I know. But he's been under too long. He's drowned by now, Elly."

She looked past Adar's shoulder and saw Aklaq on shore, surrounded by his loose dogs. "Hurry, before the ice breaks again."

Adar scooped her into his arms and ran for the embankment.

"Your shoulder!" Elice cried.

He only hitched her higher in his arms. They reached the shore that hugged the side of the mountain. She looked around for Sakari, but didn't see her. Elice had only a moment to worry for her friend before the ground pitched fiercely. Rocks broke loose from the sheer cliff, pelting the ground. Adar and Elice were thrown onto a mound of snow, Adar landing on top of her. The ground heaved beneath them, and snow forced itself into Elice's mouth. She choked, coughing and gasping for breath. Adar flipped over and scooted them both under an overhang of rock. Aklaq quickly followed. Snow shook loose from the cliff, sealing them inside.

"What was that?" Elice gasped.

"Earth tremors. They get worse every time," Aklaq said.

Elice flooded the darkness with an aurora. "Where's Sakari?"

Aklaq glanced at the aurora and then glared at the sealed-off entrance. "She went downriver, looking for Tikaani."

Elice buried her head in Adar's chest. He bit off his mittens and began checking her for injuries. "Are you hurt?"

The pain came then, an ache along her left side, spreading to her back. But it wasn't worth mentioning, not after . . . "Tikaani—my fault," Elice mumbled.

Aklaq didn't meet her gaze. "He died a warrior defending his dogs. It was a good death."

"I tried to save him, but I couldn't find him. I couldn't—" Elice choked on a sob.

"All highmen know the water means death," Aklaq said. "You saved me, and you saved Adar."

"But no one would've have been in danger in the first place if—"

"Stop!" Aklaq commanded. "Do not cheapen Tikaani's death by taking credit for it. The bravery is his." The shaking stopped abruptly, and the Svass turned away from Elice. "I'm going back for Sakari." He dug his way outside, leaving Adar and Elice alone.

"They can't swim," Adar said in awe. "Of course they can't. How could they ever learn in such frigid waters? But they still go out on those tiny kayaks and chase down whales."

Elice tried to swallow her tears. "Adar?"

He pulled her into his arms and held her so tight she thought he might be the only thing holding her together. "Quiet now. Aklaq is right. Tikaani chose to fight in the face of his fear. You did everything you could to save him."

"Your shoulder?" she managed.

"It's fine. I'm fine. Come on. We need to help Aklaq look for Sakari." Adar crawled out, Elice right behind him. Immediately, a snowstorm enveloped them. She briefly considered splitting up but remembered the wolves. What if they attacked again? She and Adar hurried along the river, frantically searching for Sakari.

"Elice," Adar said after a while, "I don't think we can make it. Not if your mother isn't above killing you as well." He hesitated a moment. "Maybe you should stop. With Aklaq and Sakari, I can get out of here on my own."

She stared at him. "You think my mother would stop hunting you simply because I stayed behind? Because I don't."

He was silent for a beat. "One of us should survive this."

Elice paused, closing her eyes to concentrate on the border between winter and summer. "We're close, Adar—so close I can feel it. I think it's just on the other side of this mountain." She glanced up to find him watching her. "If I give up now, I'll never forgive myself. I can't make you come with me. Just like you can't make me stay."

He pursed his lips and gave a curt nod. Shielding their eyes, they saw the others approaching from downstream, the dogs a huddled mass around them. Letting out a great sigh of relief, Elice hurried toward them. Sakari met her halfway, and suddenly their arms were around each other and they were both crying, snow and tears mixing on their faces. Elice ached with the loss of Tikaani and was glad for the comfort of her friend's embrace. In that moment she realized something. She had friends. People who cared about her. People who had risked their lives to help her. They were good and strong and brave—everything her mother had said they weren't.

"I'm sorry," Elice whispered, guilt stabbing her again.

"You did everything you could," Sakari whispered with a squeeze.

"How much farther do these mountains go?" Adar asked Aklaq.

"We're nearly there. We've already passed the summit. From here on out, the descent is relatively short but very steep. A day or day and a half, depending on this storm. Beyond that is the tundra where the caribou graze in the high summer."

Elice and Sakari released each other. "I think . . ." Elice bit the inside of her cheek. "If we can just get past this mountain."

"The dogs." Aklaq gestured to the injured animals around him. "They cannot pull the sled."

Elice steeled herself. It was up to her to get them to safety. "Aklaq, you have already risked so much, given so much. Stay here, let the dogs recover, and then go into the grazing grounds and hunt for your family. Sakari, stay with him. Continue on when it's safer."

Aklaq dropped his head. "As you say."

"I'm coming with you," Sakari said, her face set.

Elice reached out and touched her cheek, which was smooth and soft. "My mother's wrath isn't kindled toward you. I think she would let you go."

Sakari took Elice's outstretched hand in her own and squeezed it before releasing it. "Even after you leave winter, you will need help from the people. I can get it for you."

Elice shook her head. "I can't see you hurt. Not after today. I won't let anyone else die for me."

"You think I fear death?" Sakari snorted. "If it takes me to be with all those who died instead of me, I welcome it." She pushed past Elice and Adar.

"Come on, Elice," Adar said, and then he too trudged up the hill.

She paused and turned back, considering Aklaq. She formed a shelter of packed snow, leaving plenty of room for the dogs. "Will you be all right?" She didn't look at him as she asked, knowing that if she met his eyes, she'd completely lose hold of her emotions.

"I am strong, and I have plenty of food and a shelter. We will be fine."

It sent a pang through her to realize it was true—he would be safer without her. "Thank you," she choked out. "Tell Tikaani's family . . ." Elice couldn't finish and she turned around and made for the others, not wanting the highman to see the tears freezing to her cheeks.

19

With Adar and Sakari beside her, Elice studied the steep slope. Far below, the terrain flattened out into a never-ending plain of green that made her insides churn with longing. There was summer. They only had this one last mountain to cross. But her mother was certain to come after them with something else.

Elice pulled on winter, spreading a blanket of fluffy snow straight down as far as she could see. Then she formed three sleds of ice. "Let's outrun her." She took the first sled—she'd need to be in the lead in case she had to call upon more snow. "Steer by leaning," she told Adar and Sakari. "Jump off before you crash into anything."

Elice pushed off. Immediately, the wind tore at her loose clothes and hair. A pang of fear tore through her. She glanced back to find Sakari and Adar racing after her. She vowed to protect them with her own life if necessary.

A lone howl brought her head around. Behind them, standing above a precipice, Lowl lifted her black snout toward the sky. The precipice before the wolf began to slide, the snow sloughing off its surface. An avalanche hurtled toward the sledders, moving like water, billows of snow rising like dust.

The roar reached Elice then, the wind pushing against them from behind. Adar was shouting something, but she couldn't hear him over the rushing sound. The snow would overtake them in moments. Elice turned back to see her friends veering off the path. Thinking fast, she adjusted the slope ahead of them, making it not quite ice, but almost. She adjusted the runners, too, sharpening the edges.

All three sleds careened dangerously down the mountain, the wave of snow thundering after them. Elice concentrated, keeping the ice slick and the runners working perfectly; if either failed, she and Sakari and Adar would be overtaken.

At the base of the mountain, Elice's power over winter suddenly slipped. It was like winter was still there, but muffled instead of crisp and clear. The sleds kept going, but she had lost her wicked-fast control over snow and ice. They were at the mercy of the mountain now. The mountain and her mother.

The icy path softened, the snow turning slushy. The sleds slowed down and veered dangerously, first to one side and then the other. It took all Elice's effort to steer her sled. Then one of her runners caught an edge. She flipped and rolled down the mountain. She heard a grunt and something slammed into her, shattering when it hit. Another body was rolling with hers—Sakari, her limbs flying in every direction.

Finally, they came to a tangled halt. Moaning, Elice sat up and caught sight of Sakari's form—limp and unmoving, just as Elice's father had been those years ago. She held her trembling fingers under Sakari's nose and was relieved to feel the reassuring puffs of breath. Elice pushed herself up, slush seeping between her fingers. Adar had managed to slow his sled enough to jump off and run for them. Behind him, the avalanche was still devouring the landscape.

"Run!" he screamed. He threw an unconscious Sakari over his good shoulder. Elice shot after him, knowing they would suffocate if the rushing snow overtook them. With a deafening roar, it exploded past them, tearing shrubs from the ground with a great ripping sound.

Somehow the avalanche didn't hit them. Elice was running too fast to look back to see why. Beneath her feet, slush gave way to mud, which gave way to spongy green grass. Suddenly she knew they had left the Winter Realm.

Chest heaving, she turned to look behind them. Her mother stood, her wings spread to block the avalanche, which spread out onto the tundra all around them. The Winter Queen had spared their lives. *But I still can't trust her*, Elice thought. She stepped in front of Adar, who set down a groaning Sakari.

"Elice!" her mother called. "Please don't go." For the first time in Elice's memory, Ilyenna seemed rattled.

Elice squared herself. "You killed Tikaani. You would have killed me!"

Her mother stretched a hand toward her. "I was only trying to stop you."

Rage swelled up inside Elice, filling her so that snow flew from her lips. "Well, you failed! I am free now. I have fulfilled your bargain!"

Ilyenna's empty hand fell by her side. "He will betray you in the end."

"The world is not the evil, dark place you led me to believe it was," Elice replied, barely reining in her emotions. "And neither are its people. I have seen them—have seen their courage and goodness. If there is darkness and evil, I will face that too. But at least I won't be alone. I will have my friends by my side."

Ilyenna unfurled her great wings and pumped them to lift herself off the ground. She hovered, the snow forming a mold in the shape of her wings. "Well then, Daughter, I hope you are strong enough for the darkness. Because you won't have to go searching. It will find you."

20

Elice leapt across the large, interconnected puddles, a school of minnows darting away from her passing. Dozens of brilliant-yellow, low-growing flowers graced the gently rolling hills. She bent down to examine them, her fingers tracing the soft petals. Unable to resist, she picked one and held it to her nose, inhaling deep. It smelled herbal, almost medicinal, instead of sweet. But Elice didn't care. She had never smelled a flower that wasn't frozen. She picked two more, tucked them behind her ear, and resumed her climb up the highest hill. The mossy ground squishing up between her bare toes was much like slush, only dirtier.

"Elice, where are you going?" Adar called.

"I have to see." Had to see the land she'd always dreamed of, the land of life and color. She finally reached the top of the hill, a warm breeze tugging her loose hair over her face. She impatiently gathered it over one shoulder and looked out over the sweeping landscape, covered with small lakes and so much color it hurt her eyes. Her heart swelled with hope. This was the life before her—full of possibilities and discoveries. And best of all, she was no longer alone.

Sakari came into view below her and looked up. The other girl's head was bandaged, and she'd complained of a bad headache. But she had insisted they carry on. She pointed south and a little west, telling Elice, "That way to the coast and my village." Then Sakari started off, leaning on an antler she'd found.

Elice heard Adar scrambling up the hill, and soon he stepped up beside her. "We made it," she said as she reached out to take his hand. When he didn't answer, she turned to look at him. He stared at the Summer Realm, his face cast in shadow, his expression troubled. Why wasn't he happy?

He shook his head. "I was so focused on escaping, I didn't let myself see beyond. Didn't let myself see . . ." He turned to her, his gaze searching. "Elice, whatever happens, I want you to know I won't let anyone hurt you."

She laughed. "Hurt me? Adar, we've left the danger behind."

He stared at their intertwined fingers. "You're sure this is what you want? No matter the consequences?"

She stepped closer and cradled his cheek in her hand. "After all we've been through, you expect me to have doubts now?"

"I just want you to be sure."

She gave him a brilliant smile. "I chose this. You didn't force me." She leaned in a little, her arms spread. He embraced her, locking his arms around her as if he never wanted to let go.

With her head resting on his shoulder, she watched the snowstorm disappear—gone from one moment to the next. The sun slid behind the mountains, casting a shadow across the realm. Casting Elice in shadow. She glanced back to see it stretch on to pierce the Summer Realm like a knifepoint.

But beyond that was light. Holding Adar's hand, she stepped into that light.

Amber Argyle is the number-one bestselling author of the Witch Song Series and the Fairy Queen Series. Her books have been nominated for and won awards in addition to being translated into French and Indonesian.

Amber graduated cum laude from Utah State University with a degree in English and physical education, a husband, and a two-year old. Since then, she and her husband have added two more children, which they are actively trying to transform from crazy small people into less crazy larger people.

To receive Amber Argyle's starter library for free,
simply tell her where to send it:
http://eepurl.com/l8f1l

OTHER TITLES BY AMBER ARGYLE

Witch Song Series

Witch Song
Witch Born
Witch Rising
Witch Fall

Fairy Queens Series

Of Ice and Snow
Winter Queen
Of Fire and Ash
Summer Queen
Of Sand and Storm
Daughter of Winter
Winter's Heir

www.ingramcontent.com/pod-product-compliance
Lightning Source LLC
Chambersburg PA
CBHW060146130626
46556CB00006B/2513